The Country
of Loneliness

a novel

Dawn Paul

MARICK
PRESS

Library of Congress Cataloguing in Publication Data

Dawn Paul
The Country of Loneliness

ISBN 978-1-934851-07-4

Copyright © by Dawn Paul, 2009
Design and typesetting by Sean Tai
Cover design by Sean Tai

Printed and bound in the United States

Marick Press
P.O. Box 36253
Grosse Pointe Farms
Michigan 48236
www.marickpress.com

Mariela Griffor, Publisher

Distributed by
Small Press Distribution
and
Wayne State University Press

This book is for my father

ACKNOWLEDGMENTS

I would like to thank Rebecca Brown for her care and wisdom in editing this book, and Mariela Griffor for all her work at Marick Press. I am also grateful to writers Sarah Getty, Ann Killough, Elizabeth Rollins and Christine Simokaitis for reading early versions of this book.

Thank you to the Vermont Studio Center and the Ragdale Foundation for time and peace.

Special thanks, as always, to Marilyn McCrory.

The Country
of Loneliness

I DON'T DREAM OF my father.

But shortly after his death, he appeared in a series of dreams I had while driving across the country. I was twenty-one then. I had planned the trip before he died and left as soon as possible after his death. Throughout that journey, away from the effort of trying to piece my mother's life back together, of trying to help her through a deep grief I did not share or understand, I dreamed of my father every night.

The dreams were remarkable for being ordinary. In them, I am sitting with my father at a table. Maybe we are drinking coffee, maybe having a cigarette. I smoked then, but seldom in dreams. There is a companionable quiet between us. We talk very little. We offer each other more coffee. Remark on the weather. Sometimes my father is reading the newspaper, the kind of reading that is a shared activity. He comments on the news, reads pieces of articles aloud to me, holds out a page to show me a photo. It is the very ordinariness of these scenes that makes them so compelling. This quiet time with my father. Time I never had with him in life. He is an ordinary man in these dreams, enjoying his daughter's company. My company. I like him.

This man calm and in control of himself. This is what I always wanted from him – ordinary time. Peace. No more than that. Not even love. In my short years with him, I would have traded the love he had for me for the small pleasures of ordinary peace.

Each night, all across the country, on mountains, in deserts, and finally, along the Pacific coast, I dreamed quiet, companionable dreams of my father, Philip. I awoke happy and refreshed as I traveled further and further from home. For many years, I considered them my period of mourning.

Morning, 1939. The sun is rising over the hills above the valley. The clouds are pink underneath, the sky above them light blue. The mill by the river is quiet, crouched like a big cat with the morning sun on its red bricks. The bricks are rosy and alive. Easy to believe, young Philip thinks, that God made mankind from clay.

It is so quiet that Philip hears the fierce scratching of the sparrows under Mrs. Nason's hedge. The sun is above the eastern hills now and turns the western hills red-gold. Philip whistles an exclamation at the beauty of it all. "WHEE-WHEW!"

"I will always remember this. The red-gold light on the hills. The cool fall air on my face. The quiet." He does not really think these words or say them. Only the whistle.

Philip has just turned sixteen. It is the first time he has noticed a sunrise, stopped to watch the light come up. It is the first time he has held a memory as his alone. He thinks that years from now he will be able to describe this morning, to rekindle his joy at its beauty. Whee-whew! The warmth of the sun on his face as he stood in the street. The sparrows busily scratching in the dirt. But no one ever asks, did you

3

ever watch the sun rise? So he never tells anyone that he stood in the street and thought about God and clay.

There will be other sunrises. Some will be glorious, after an endless and terrible night at sea. In time, he will have only the idea of a sunrise, not this one morning in October. But for now, he has this, and it is enough. Soon there will be everything that came after.

I DON'T KNOW WHEN I began to not know my father. There was a time when I did. A time when I saw him the way other people did, and the way everyone seemed to remember him after he died. The big man with a loud laugh, generous and jolly with ruddy, red cheeks. When I was two years old, I knew that man.

Scenes from that time remain in my memory in round circles that fade at the edges, round balls of time and place, like the clear glass bulb on the Christmas tree with snow and a little red house inside. In the round globe of the bedroom that I share with my brothers, my mother dresses me one winter day and buttons my coat. She drives to where Daddy works, the Navy base. This is where the doctor is, where we go to get polio shots and groceries at the Commissary. A man at the gate smiles into the car window and salutes. I salute back and he laughs. My mother drives through the gates to a white building and we hurry to the door because it is a cold day. Inside, it's big, lit with colored lights, with high shelves full of all kinds of things. We walk between the shelves and then there is a bright circle of gold light. In the

5

very middle of this circle, in a huge chair, is Santa Claus. Everything outside the circle fades.

My mother leans down and whispers in my ear, "Go see Santa, go sit on his lap," and I go. I am fearless. Santa is smiling down at me. He has a shiny white beard and a soft red suit. He helps me climb up on his lap.

"HO HO HO What Do You Want For Christmas Little Girl?"

I look up at Santa's face. Above the soft white beard are dark, slightly slanted eyes and red, shiny skin with tiny, squiggly red lines. I reach up and touch that warm, red skin. It's Daddy. It makes fine sense to me. Daddy is always Santa Claus. Not the real Santa Claus who lives at the North Pole, but a kind of everyday Santa Claus. And today Daddy is dressed up like Santa. I'm not sure I'm supposed to know that this Santa Claus is Daddy. He doesn't say anything about it, calls me Little Girl like he doesn't know me. I think we're pretending so I pretend to not know him. I tell him what I want for Christmas. Blocks. "What Else? A Dolly?" he says. I nod yes, watch his sparkly eyes, his smile under the shiny white beard. When I slide off his lap and go back to my mother, I whisper, "That was Daddy." She looks surprised and asks how I know this. "I saw his skin," I tell her.

I find out there is no Santa of any kind after my father leaves the Navy and we move to a new house. This house has separate bedrooms for me and my brothers. My parents' bedroom has a big closet with sliding doors. On a winter day when my mother is in the basement washing clothes and my father is at work or maybe at a bar, I step into their room. I tell myself that I am going to slide the closet door just for the fun of it – it's the only sliding door I've ever seen and I like to play with it.

The Robertson kids next door say there is no Santa. My brothers, who are older than me, tell me that there is. They insist they heard him on the roof last Christmas Eve. I want to believe my brothers, but I have, already, a scientific mind. I have been gathering evidence. The world is a big place to circle in one night with flying reindeer, and I have traced our chimney down to the little boxy furnace in the basement. I'm afraid of what I will find in my parents' closet.

My father was not Santa at the Navy base this year. Instead, he sat at the kitchen table with his bottle of beer and called me to sit on his lap. He hollered "HO HO HO, What Do You Want For Christmas Little Girl," and I pretended he was Santa though he smelled like beer and cigarettes and was not dressed like Santa. I asked for skis. He said, "What Else?" but I wanted to get away from the smell of beer and smoke, so I said I just wanted skis.

Now, I slide the closet door open. There are our presents, piled on the floor, leaning into my mother's coats and dresses, stacked high up on a shelf.

I see my new skis leaning in the back corner of the closet. Beautiful little blue skis with wooden poles. I am sorry I slid the closet door open, that the skis will not be a surprise. But it's a relief to finally know for sure.

On Christmas morning I open my eyes and run down the hall to the living room. It's full of our presents, a huge pile spilling out from under the tree. I see the chess and checker set that was up on the closet shelf and the wooden baseball bat that was leaning against my mother's good dress in its plastic wrap. There is the football that was on the floor next to my father's shoes. My skis stick out from under the tree. I am happy to see them, but wish I could still imagine they were delivered late at night while I was sleeping.

My brothers and I poke at the gifts and wait for Santa to get up and hand them out. I find a book about dinosaurs that I hadn't seen in the closet and am happy to have one surprise.

My father comes down the hall shouting MERRY CHRISTMAS! He goes to the kitchen to get a beer and starts handing out the presents. He is beaming, watching us dive into our presents, popping open another bottle of beer, then another. I pretend that everything is a surprise. When he says, "Was Santa Good To You This Year?" I say yes. I do not say there is no Santa. That would ruin the day for everyone, but especially, I think, for him. He tells me to go get Santa another beer and my mother makes a face. She says we need to start picking up all this stuff. But my father opens his beer and sits back on the couch, smiling.

"I have everything I want for Christmas," he says, and he starts crying and wiping his eyes. "Don't worry. I'm not crying because I'm sad, I'm crying because I'm happy." My stomach clenches a little. My father's crying does not seem real, like he's really happy or even sad. It makes my father seem like a big stranger, sitting in our living room, blowing his nose and opening another bottle of beer.

There is not much snow in the yard, but I take my skis outside and attach them to my red rubber boots. They have straps with laces and metal springs that go around my heels. At the top of the little hill behind the house, I crouch like the ski racers on TV, then push off and go sliding down into the Robertson's yard and fall. I get up, push off again with the wooden poles, and slide down another little hill into the woods behind the back yard. I pole myself along a path crusted with thin snow, over leaves and sticks and chunks of ice. It starts to snow, tiny flakes that catch on the fuzz on the back of my mittens. I think of the song that my mother sometimes sings, "I'm Dreaming of a White Christmas." The woods are quiet. I am skiing. The Christmas feeling, the glowing something-wonderful-is-going-to-happen feeling, comes over me like the new snow.

When I go back into the house, my parents are in the kitchen making Christmas dinner. My father is yelling at my mother. He has dropped a big pan of something on the floor and is blaming her. She is saying she'll clean it up, and I wish I was brave enough to say that it isn't fair for her to clean it, he dropped it.

The living room is empty. My brothers have taken their presents into their bedroom, except the football which is huddled under the tree. The coffee table still has my mother's half-full cup of tea and my father's beer bottles on it. I count six bottles. They smell and I'd like to take them out to the garage. But I would have to walk through the kitchen again and I don't want to do that. My father is still yelling and banging pots and pans around. "You can't do anything right," he keeps saying to my mother. It isn't true, my mother does a lot of things right. She doesn't leave stinking bottles in the living room on Christmas Day.

I take my new book about dinosaurs from under the tree to my bedroom and try to read, but I can still hear the yelling in the kitchen. When my father cries, it is always the beginning of a ruined day, even if it's Christmas. I look out the window to watch the snow, but it has turned to rain.

PHILIP MADE A FRIEND one summer, one he would never forget. His pal, The Captain.

The Captain was a Rhode Island Red rooster. His red-brown feathers were the color of Philip's hair. His father warned Philip not to make a pet of The Captain. But on sticky August nights, in that long stretch between supper and bedtime, the rooster started coming around. He pecked at Philip's feet and stared up at him, head cocked, a golden eye staring straight into Philip's own.

Philip thought chickens were stupid, the way they pecked in the hot sun all day and wandered underfoot, the steady burble of their clucking like rain in a gutter. But The Captain had a gleam in his eye. Maybe intelligence, maybe just stupidity and greed. So Philip lured him with bits of corn and in time the rooster let him run his hand across his bright feathers. Then, either for more corn or to better keep him company, the bird leapt up on the back of Philip's wrist. He pressed his scaly claws into Philip's skin.

By the end of August, The Captain – what better name for this bossy, headstrong bird – would ride on Philip's shoulder, his dark red feathers mixing with Philip's hair. Ma, of course, wouldn't have a pet in the house. Not even a dog or a cat. So Philip walked around doing his outside chores with The Captain on his shoulder. When Pa walked into the yard at the end of the day, he'd see The Captain on his son's shoulder and say, "You're going to get a hard lesson."

The Captain was moody. Some days he would sulk under the raspberry bush and watch the hens scrabble for the corn Philip put out for him. Other days he would meet Philip at the gate when he came home from school. Philip walked home everyday thinking about what mood The Captain might be in. He'd round the corner hoping to see The Captain standing on the gatepost, straining his feathered neck to look up the road. The Captain knew what time school let out. Philip wondered what else he knew.

One Saturday, Philip's little sister May shyly handed him a gift. It was a tiny hat she had stitched out of gray felt. A little fedora. She had even made a band out of a scrap of red grosgrain ribbon. It was a very distinguished looking hat. Philip squatted down and held out his arm – his signal, his request, to The Captain to climb up on his shoulder. The Captain hopped up and May reached out to put the hat on his head. But he raised the blood-red comb on the top of his head and frightened her. Philip took the little hat.

"Easy, fella, easy . . ." He set it on The Captain's head. The Captain shook his head, which only tilted the hat at a jaunty angle. Then he seemed to forget it was there. It was one of those times when Philip had the traitorous thought that The Captain might not be that smart after all. But the fedora, tilted to the left, was perfect. The Captain was no longer a sea captain or an infantry captain. He was grander than that. He was a Captain of Industry. A maker of cities. A Carnegie, a Rockefeller. Rich, shrewd, arrogant. Cocksure.

Philip and May laughed. They couldn't help it. True to style, The Captain didn't flinch. He stood his ground and glared at them until they stopped under his commanding gaze. Then Pa banged open the gate with the black look in his eyes. May scuttled into the house and Philip reached out to grab the little hat. The Captain dodged under the porch, still wearing the hat. But Pa had seen.

"You're going to get a hard lesson – soon," he said.

Philip looked under the porch for the little fedora but it was gone.

November came and it was cold, the sun set long before supper time. Philip came home from school and sat with The Captain on the back steps. He felt the cold through the thin cloth on the seat of his pants. He had grown another inch and his pants were too short. The boys at school laughed and called them "high-waders." They were good fellows, just teasing, but he hated when they called down the halls, "Here comes Rusty in his high-waders!"

Pa walked through the gate, bent down as he passed and made an ugly snipping gesture at The Captain's neck. Philip smoothed The Captain's feathers and murmured, "We won't let that happen, will we?" The Captain cocked his head and looked up at Philip. The light from the kitchen shone in his gold eye. The Captain looked shrewd and cunning. He looked like he had a plan to save his own neck.

But Philip had a nervous certainty that The Captain had no notion of the future, or of anything really, beyond cracked corn and the hens in the yard. He looked into The Captain's bright eye and thought of how the bird waited for him on the gatepost. But he knew that he did not believe strongly enough in The Captain. The Captain looked away and hopped down to peck at bits of straw in the square light from the kitchen window. Philip reached down to pet him.

"You're still my good pal, Captain."

The day before Thanksgiving, Pa came through the gate stamping his feet and slapping his hands together. A hard frost had come that week and the ground seemed to ring under Pa's work boots. He came into the house, took off his jacket and bent to the sink to wash his face, neck and hands. He put out his hand and Ma wordlessly handed him a clean rag. He wiped his face and said to Philip, "I've been telling you not to make a pet out of that bird. It's meat for the table."

Philip looked to Ma for appeal but she set her lips in a firm line and turned back to the stove. Pa looked at him and Philip knew that he wanted him to beg. Then Philip saw something else in his eyes. Pa wanted something from Philip and, for the first time, was not sure that he would get it. Permission. Or maybe forgiveness.

Philip banged out the door and ran to the chicken coop. The hens were tucked down in their boxes. The Captain was in his usual spot up by the roof. Philip reached up and lifted him down from his perch. He held him in his arms for a minute, but The Captain didn't like it and leapt to his shoulder. The hens stirred and made their soft kuck-kuck-kuck sounds. The Captain stretched out his wings and hopped back up to his perch. He wanted to sleep. Philip walked back to the house.

Pa never cooked or had anything to do with making meals. But on Thanksgiving morning, whether Ma refused or out of his own meanness, Pa took the cleaver and went out to the yard. It was raining big gray bullets that became sleet then rain again. Philip wiped the fog from his bedroom window and looked down into the yard. Pa walked bare-headed in the icy rain across the yard and into the coop. He walked out with The Captain clamped under one arm. He walked over to the gate post and laid The Captain's neck across it. Philip felt his stomach heave and ran downstairs to the toilet. He rinsed his mouth and put on his jacket and cap. Ma and his sisters, Ruby and May, looked at him, stricken. They didn't speak. But they'd all eat their dinner, Philip thought, though little May might choke on the meat.

Pa came in holding The Captain upside-down by the legs. The cleaver was washed clean by the rain. Philip brushed by him and ran out the door.

He wanted to run far, far away. But the cold rain soaked through his jacket even as he ran across the yard to the shed. He went inside and sat on a crate and cried. A hard lesson. He wasn't sure what he was supposed to have learned.

Philip sat in the shed all Thanksgiving day. He imagined them at their meal. Ruby and May with their heads bent to their plates. Ma going back and forth to the stove. Pa half-drunk, careless with his knife and fork, talking too loud to fill up the silence he created. Philip's place at the table, empty.

He went into the house when the lights were out and he knew they were all in bed. He did not want to see them. His throat was raw from crying and being sick to his stomach. He was shivering and hungry but walked quickly through the dark kitchen. His head and stomach felt airy and hollow and he was slightly feverish.

He was sick for several days and stayed upstairs in bed. Ma brought him tea and he saw no one else. By the time he came back downstairs, the day, the meal, and even his help-less fury, seemed part of the fever-dreams that had whirled through his days of restless, broken sleep.

I AM STANDING IN the kitchen of the first house I remember. The floor is big black and white squares, the counters are way up high.

The house is on a little dead-end street next to a two-lane highway. There are always, even when I wake late at night, the sounds of trucks and cars. We lived in another house once, a house on a Navy base. My mother says she loved that house, but I do not remember it. It was brand-new. When I was born, I was brought home from the hospital to that clean, bright house. My father was sent overseas for the first nine months of my life, my mother says. When he came home, he was so happy that he shined the wooden floors and polished all the furniture. Now, she says, he never lifts a finger. Now, there is only this house, with its cement slab porch, the huff and hiss of truck brakes, the clothesline in the back yard, the stone wall and the big empty field behind it. This is the world.

Maryclaire lives in the house next door. She is in high school, a person between kids and adults, my parents and my brothers. She drives a car, she rollerskates. Sometimes my mother asks her to take me for a walk. One day

Maryclaire takes me to the graveyard that is in the corner of the big field and shows me the smooth stones in neat rows. She tells me they are called headstones, and says if we lift the stones we will see the heads of the dead. She is trying to scare me, her eyes are wide and she smiles a toothy smile. But I want to see the heads of the dead and try to lift a stone. A boy is there, leaning on a big stone, smoking a cigarette. Maryclaire says he is our little secret, ok? The air buzzes and hums in the sun and I want to come back, so I say ok.

Except for Maryclaire, there are no other kids on the street. Mrs. Dillon lives by herself and has chickens, but I am not allowed to go there because she says I chase the chickens. I did, but only once. The Slatterys live at the end of the street, but my mother tells me to stay away from them, they're not good people.

When my brothers are in school, I play in the yard by myself. There are kids across the highway, but I am too little to cross with all the cars and big trucks. When my brothers come home from school, my mother tells them to play with me, that I am lonesome all day. Once in a while they do, but mostly they go play football with boys from school. My mother says she will be glad when my father retires from the Navy so we can buy a house and there will be other little girls for me to play with. I wonder what that will be like. I don't know any little girls.

I like playing in the yard all day. Mostly, I play pretend. I pretend to be one of the bad Slatterys and hide behind bushes to rob people. I pretend to be robbed. I dig in the dirt and pretend that I am digging for the heads of the dead. I walk on the stone wall that runs between the back yard and the field, and pretend it is a ship like my father's ship overseas and that the field is the ocean.

My father is a Chief in the Navy. Yesterday he came back from overseas and my mother and brothers and I went to bring him home. We saw his ship, a battleship, tucked between two thin ships called destroyers. His ship was huge and gray with strings of little red flags. Its long, snouty guns pointed up into the sky. My father came down a long metal stairway, wearing a white jacket with rows of gold buttons and carrying a big bag, a duffel bag. He was laughing and my mother was crying. He put the duffel bag in the trunk of the car and drove us home.

When we got home, my father stood in the middle of the kitchen and opened the duffel bag. He had presents from overseas. My brothers each got a wooden puppet and I got a bracelet with a gold heart. My brothers made their puppets fight each other and one's arm broke off. There wasn't anything to do with the bracelet, and my mother put it away for when I got older. My father lifted me up to the ceiling and said he was glad to be home.

Today he is still home and I am in the kitchen instead of playing in the yard. My mother is at the stove cooking something in a big black frying pan. My father comes into the kitchen, holding the car keys. My mother asks where he is going and he says don't start and then they both yell at each other. My father slams the car keys on the counter and holds his empty hands in front of him. He is still yelling, but my mother is looking at his hands. She is in the corner between the stove and the counter. Her eyes go back and forth but her feet have nowhere to go. My father rushes at her, yells, and pushes her. A glass falls off the counter and breaks on the floor. That seems to stop everything. My father leaves the room and I hear him banging around in my parents' bedroom. My mother sweeps the glass into a dustpan with a little broom. She is crying, but not the way she cried when my father came off the ship. I stand still so they will not see me.

My father comes back into the kitchen, grabs the car keys and rushes outside. My mother follows, still holding the little broom. Now that my father is not in the house, it is okay to move, and I go out the door. My father is walking across the grass to the car and my mother is yelling at him but he doesn't answer. She throws the little broom. It flies slowly through the air, spinning end over end, then hits my father right on the back of his neck. I am amazed that my mother does this, amazed that the broom hits him so perfectly. I want to clap my hands and yell. But I am afraid my father will turn around, come back and hit her some more and maybe hit me for clapping. He just keeps walking, does not even turn his head, and gets in the car. He is not hurt. I realize he cannot be hurt. That is only for my mother and me.

He drives down the highway, leaves us standing alone in the yard. I run to get the broom and bring it back to my mother. I want to show her that I can help her. She thanks me and wipes her eyes. She cries and says, "He can't even stay home for five minutes." I wish we were the ones driving away from this house. But he gets to drive away. We are left here, my mother and me, alone next to the highway.

PHILIP LIVES ON a narrow street lined with houses that used to belong to the mill, back when the mill was trying to lure young men and women from farms in the valley. The front of the house is close to the street, with just a strip of weedy ground between the stone foundation and the sidewalk. A rose, a rambler rose his mother calls it, twines around the wooden trellis that is nailed to the shingles between the parlor window and the front door. No one uses the front door. Everyone, even peddlers and religious ladies with free pamphlets, walks down the street behind the house to the gate in the high board fence.

Philip is almost twelve years old, alone in the back yard on a July afternoon. He has his eye against a hole in the high board fence. He is waiting, cocks his head, listening to the voices of two boys coming up the sidewalk, Allie Wodecki and Chet Peiczarka. He leaps up, grabs the top of the fence and hauls himself up until he is looking over the top, his feet braced against the boards. He sees that Chet has a rubber ball, is tossing it in the air as he walks.

"Hey!"

"Hay is for horses, but better for cows!"

"Where're you going?"

"No place. To play catch. Come on. We'll play three-way."

"Can't. I have to stay in the yard."

"Are you being punished? What did you do?"

("Lay off. His old lady makes him stay in the yard.")

"Let's play catch right here, fellas."

"Here?"

"Yeah, over the fence."

"That's no good. We can't do fly balls or grounders."

"We can do pop-ups. C'mon –" Philip lets go of the fence, drops down and stands looking up, cupping his hands, waiting.

"C'mon – throw!"

On the other side of the fence, Chet pockets the ball and winks at Allie.

"Stand way back, Rusty!" Chet and Allie grin. "Way back now . . ." On the other side, Philip steps backwards, looking up at the top of the fence, hands held out, ready. Chet and Allie step away quietly.

"Way back, Rusty." They walk softly down the sidewalk. Philip waits. Then drops his hands, knows he's been fooled.

"Stupid jerks!" He bows his head, wipes his nose with the back of his hand. Then he leaps at the fence, grabs, pulls himself up. "Hey – you jerks!"

Chet and Allie look back. Chet waves, they both laugh. Philip wants to hurt them, pound on them, make them cry. But they are too far away. Then he remembers what Pa called Mr. Wodecki one night, he cannot remember why.

"Polacks! Stupid, dirty Polacks!"

The next time Chet walks by alone, Philip is ready. He stands with his face against an opening made by a broken slat. He has a penny in his pocket from Uncle Omer, Ma's quiet bachelor brother.

"Hey Chet – c'mere."

"I can't. I need to get home."

"Just one minute."

"Can't." He leans in to whisper. ("I need to take a leak.")

"No you don't. Hey. Will anyone ever be better than Babe Ruth?"

"Heck no. No one will ever beat the Babe."

"Nobody?"

"I got to go. See you in school."

"Wait. I'll give you a penny."

Chet stops, astounded. "A penny?"

"No fooling. A penny."

"You ain't got a penny." (He's peering through the broken slat. Philip can see one blue eye with stubby, blond lashes.)

"Do too." Philip holds it up to Chet's eye.

"Give it to me!" Chet pokes two fingers through the broken slat. Philip steps back.

"You have to talk first. Why's Ruth the best?"

"He's the best hitter. Ever. A genuine slugger."

"I guess he's my favorite, too."

They stand for a while, on either side of the fence, hands in their pockets. Philip's face is strained, like he's trying to think of something else to say. He leans and looks through the slat. Chet picks at a scab on his elbow.

"How did you cut your arm?"

Chet shrugs, pulls his sleeve back down. "I dunno. I must of fell. You going to give me my penny?"

Philip can think of nothing else to say. He sticks the penny out through the slot. Chet takes it, looks at it with awe.

"Thanks, Rusty. You're a swell guy." Chet runs down the street. Philip watches through the broken slat for a long while after Chet has gone. Ruby comes out of the house carrying a basket of laundry.

"Help me hang these." She's fourteen and bossy. He turns on her, head down, fists balled up.

"I don't have to."

"Well you're just standing there –"

"Leave me alone! I'll stand here if I want!"

Ruby drops the basket and walks up to him, stands face-to-face. "Don't you talk to me like that. What's the matter with you, anyway?"

He will not let her see him cry. He's too big for that now and she has seen him cry too often. He shoves her aside and runs to the shed.

MY FAVORITE PLACE to eat is Buffalo Bob's Burger Barn. Sometimes my father gives my mother money and she takes us there for burgers and fries. But tonight my father is buying plates of fish and chips to take home, which is a rare treat, even better than burgers. There aren't many customers, and Buffalo Bob himself takes my father's order and yells it back to the kitchen. Buffalo Bob is big, almost as big as my father and is loud like my father, too.

"Hey buddy, how's business?" my father roars.

Buffalo Bob roars back, "Can't keep any help. Nobody wants to work these days." He slaps the shiny counter with a white rag to show that he is willing to work.

My father says there must be kids at the high school who need a job, but Buffalo Bob says even his own kids don't want to work. "They don't know how good they've got it. What they need," he says, "is another Depression."

"Jeepers, buddy, don't wish that on them," my father says. He gives a little shiver, and it looks comical to see such a big, loud man shake like he's afraid. Then our order is ready, each plate slipped into its own greasy bag, a stack of plates smelling like heaven.

Back in the car, my father tells me he can't believe Buffalo Bob would wish another Depression on his own kids. "I'll tell you what the Depression was like," he says. And I know he is going to tell me, once again, the story of the beancounters. I don't find the story very frightening, but when my father tells it, he shivers like he did when Buffalo Bob wished for another Depression. He tells this story to me and my brothers whenever we complain. I think he must tell it to himself everyday.

"When I was a kid," he starts, as always, "it was The Depression. Times were bad for everybody." He tells me this like I've never heard it before. "I remember walking by a neighbor's house. Their door was open and I could see inside. The kids were sitting around the kitchen table. The father was counting out beans as he put them on their plates, one by one. Counting beans onto his kids' plates. And his kids sitting there, watching."

I see a boy my age, watching. Just after sunset, on his way home for supper. The light was on in their kitchen, a bare bulb over the table. The family gathered 'round, boys in overalls, girls in worn cotton dresses. He turned to look and caught them in this shameful and private moment. He watched with pity that was part revulsion, like the way I felt the day I found six baby rabbits drowned in the river behind our house. This family, so hungry, yet so like his own. Not Dustbowl farmers or starving Chinese peasants.

And the kids sitting there watching. My father always repeats that.

My father, on his way home, glimpsing a possible future through an open door. Not knowing, as I do from reading history books, that the Depression would come to an end. He tells this story to me to make me grateful for my easy life. To scare me and to promise me that I do not need to be afraid.

He doesn't say anything else, just drives. I sit looking out the window at the stores on Tiogue Avenue, the crispy brown smell of fish and chips filling the car. I try to see myself as one of the beancounter's kids, watching another bean get added to my plate. A scene as far removed from my life as Eskimos eating whale blubber. When my father tells this story, I know he sees himself doling out those beans as his hungry children watch, a failure as a man and breadwinner.

My father takes his role as breadwinner seriously. He talks about feeding the kids, getting the kids fed. Other parents do not talk like that, as though children are livestock. We bring in the plates of hot fish and chips and he stands over the kitchen table watching us eat, hands on his hips, his broad, red face shining. The pride of full plates.

"Have some more. There's plenty here."

I do not have even a passing acquaintance with true hunger. I take for granted this miracle of bountiful food. What I want is money to go to Girl Scout camp this summer. I also need a new bathing suit. My mother says mine has gotten so tight it's embarrassing. I wish for things like a complete set of the Nancy Drew mystery books, not three meals a day.

What I want is to not be the one who is always sent to my father for anything we need besides food. My family is not poor like the beancounters. We have money, but my father owns it, decides how it is spent. If I need a winter jacket or money to go on a school field trip, my mother braids my hair so I look nice and signals when he is in a good mood. Then I walk up to him and ask. It is understood that I can get away with asking, he will not yell at me or hit me. But I am afraid every time.

Every time I ask my father for money, I remember a hot day when I was very young. We lived in the first house then, the house on the highway, so I must have been about three. My mother took me for a long walk. There were weeds along the roadside and sidewalks with broken cement. It was dusty and trucks went by. We went to a place on a corner, a bar. I had probably been to the bar with my father, had sat on a stool eating redskin peanuts and drinking a soda while he had a few beers. It was not an unfamiliar place. Even now, I remember the grainy smell of beer, of whiskey and men's sweat.

My mother smoothes my hair and sends me in. It is dark and cool inside. There is a row of stools along the bar with shiny metal legs and above the bar, a long silvery mirror. My father leans against the bar in a bright, white shirt, laughing with other men. He looks down at me and smiles, surprised. His teeth are as white as his shirt. I say to him what my mother told me to say. It is a request for money, but I don't really know that. Only that I am asking for something because she does not want to ask. The other men laugh.

My father takes my hand and leads me outside where my mother waits on the sidewalk. He shouts at her, shoves her against a car. I'm afraid he will hurt her. He says to never do this again. "How Dare You Send a Kid In." This is not, I know, what my mother thought would happen. I think I am not going to be sent to him again and I'm glad.

Now when my father tells the story about the family gathered around the table watching beans counted onto their plates, part of me envies their honest poverty. They had no money. It wasn't something that was there but out of reach, spent on drink, endlessly argued over. I resent the hungry beancounters as well as the frightened boy who witnessed them. That this family is held up to me as the might-have-been.

MY OLDEST BROTHER is ready to go to the high school prom. He's wearing a rented tuxedo and my mother is trying to pin a red carnation onto his black satin lapel. My other brother is snapping pictures. The dog is barking and jumping. My job in all this commotion, as my mother calls it, is to hold the box with the corsage and make sure my brother does not leave the house without it.

My father sits on the couch, watching. "How much were those flowers?" he asks. My brother mutters that he doesn't remember. "It's a lot of money," my father says. "Tuxedo, tickets, flowers. How do the poor kids afford it?"

My brother looks a him for minute, puzzled. Then he says there aren't any.

"What do you mean?" my father says.

"There aren't any poor kids in our school." My oldest brother looks to my other brother, who agrees that this is true.

"There are always poor kids. I quit school because I couldn't afford a pair of pants. The school should start some kind of a charity fund for them, so they can go to the prom. You boys should start one."

My brothers shrug and will not look at my father. They both act like they are in a hurry, though only one of them is going anywhere tonight. They tell him that no one would use the fund, that no kid at school needs it or would admit to needing it.

"There's no shame to being poor," my father says. "You can be poor, but not dirty." But my brothers are not listening. They are trying to get the dog to pose with my brother in his tuxedo. My father shakes his head. It is both a pride and a frustration to him that his kids know nothing about being poor, that they are ashamed when he even says the word. Poor.

I MAGINE.

Sunday at St. John the Baptist, 1939. I slip into the pew next to him, my father, Philip. This is before he left home, before he went to war. A Catholic church, the French-Canadian parish. Philip shifts over. Skinny boy, all wrists and ankles sticking out of frayed cuffs. There's no older brother to supply hand-me-downs. His father's clothes are still too big for him. His father's wrists and ankles are knobby and hard like the roots of an oak. His father refuses to go to church.

Philip kneels and places his grubby boy's fingers together like a steeple. Dirt under his fingernails even on Sunday, but not for lack of scrubbing.

"You can be poor, but not dirty." He hopes his mother does not see.

The priest on his altar turns to face the congregation. He leaves off the sing-song Latin

et cum spiritu tu o-oh

and speaks plain English, the sermon. He talks about the poor:

The Poor will go straight to Heaven.

Blessed are The Poor.

Pray for The Poor. We must pray for The Poor.

The Poor sit in front of him, cardboard cut to patch the soles of their shoes. Too ashamed to let the collection basket slide under their noses without tossing in a nickel. Philip tosses his coin and wants to snatch it back as soon as it leaves his fingers. His eyes follow the basket as it's whisked to the next pew and the next, like watching his cap swirl down the river and sink. Blessed are The Poor.

Philip wonders what Father Michaud knows about cold-chapped hands and socks darned thick at the heel and toe. Does Father Michaud unwrap a lard sandwich at lunchtime and bolt it down before anyone sees? No, and neither does God.

Philip looks at his mother, her head bowed, her eyes closed.

If she's praying, she's got a lot to pray for.

If she's praying, it's the same prayer as last Sunday and the Sunday before because nothing in her life has gotten any better that Philip can see.

Pray for The Poor.

Philip looks at his dirty fingernails steepled before his face. Why doesn't God listen when The Poor pray for themselves?

PHILIP IS ALMOST SIXTEEN. He wakes from a dream. Was it early or late? Saturday morning, the sky an even gray behind the bare branches of the oak tree outside his bedroom window. He was warm under the blanket, his own heat saved up all night. But the tip of his nose was cold, sticking out of the blanket. He crossed his eyes to look at his nose, summer freckles still there. The wool blanket was prickly against his cheek and jaw and he moved his face against it to feel the roughness. He slid his hand up to his jaw and rubbed along the bone, smooth. He wished it was rough like the blanket. Almost sixteen – what if his beard never grows in?

All the fellows at school said that shaving made your beard grow in faster. He thought of his father's straight razor, open like a jackknife, dried soap and bits of whisker on it. He was afraid to use it, would end up slitting his throat. Then Pa would knock him around for taking it. He'd watched his father scrape his throat with it, pulling the loose skin on his face this way and that. Philip touched his own throat, the skin so thin he could feel the ridges of his windpipe underneath, and tried to imagine laying a razor against it.

It grew light enough to see the wood across the slant of the ceiling above his bed. Pa had whitewashed Ruby and May's room, but never got around to doing his. He was glad. He liked to study the patterns in the bare wood grain. There was a man with a blocky nose winking at him, a begging dog he'd named Jocko. Directly over his head, the wood grain swirled around a knot, like water around a stone in the river.

Summer nights when he was little and put to bed before dark, he had discovered these friends and places in the wood. They were familiar now, and his alone. Once he had tried to show Jocko to May, but she would not follow his pointing finger, would only look out the window. He figured she had her own world and did not need his.

He poked his head out of the blankets like a turtle and strained his ears across the hall. Shuffles and rustlings came from Ruby and May's room.

"Leave it, May!"

Philip winced. How could Ruby speak so sharply to May? Like being mean to a sparrow.

"That's your Sunday dress – leave it!"

May always tried to sneak into her prettiest clothes, even on Saturday, the day for their most raggedy clothes. If Ruby or Ma didn't catch her, May would wear her Sunday dress or shiny shoes in the muddy yard. She had no notion of saving anything. She wanted the prettiest always.

Philip wore his best clothes as little as possible, trying to make them last. Even with his everyday clothes, he was always careful to not catch and pull the buttons on his shirt cuffs. He tried to remember to never get down on one knee to tie a shoelace or shoot marbles. But still the knees of his pants wore thin and, worse, the seat of his pants. Two shiny little circles, an embarrassment on each cheek. When they wore through, Ma patched them. She patched them neatly and always tried to match the cloth. But they were patches. What good was it to ace an algebra test or take first place in the hundred-yard dash, when the losers could point to the patches on the backside of his pants? What girl would walk with a boy who wore pants with one patch covering each cheek? Even now, lying alone in bed, he felt his whole body flush with a shame so hot he threw back the blanket to feel the good cold air.

Some mornings he woke from dreams of new pants. Of opening the cupboard in his room and finding it full. White flannels. Sturdy gray wool. Blue-green plaid. Linen pants for summer. Striped seersucker. Pants with deep pockets, sharp creases, generous cuffs. The good feel of hefty new cloth. Pants – he'd wake rubbing his thumb against his fingers, feeling the cloth in his dreams.

I AM ALMOST SIXTEEN, a sophomore in high school. Worn out jeans are the fashion, at least among the kids in the art classes, the freaky, pot-smoking kids. Which is mostly what I am. I wear the same jeans every day. They have worn into the shape of my body, the indigo faded, the cuffs frayed to threads. The knees have worn out, and one night I patch them with big clumsy patches, the stitching loose and uneven. I refuse to take home ec as an elective. I choose French and art classes instead. My sewing is a mess.

In the morning, my father is sitting at the kitchen table with a cup of coffee and the newspaper, ready to go to work. He is showered and shaved and smells like sweet cologne. He looks up as I walk by, sees the patches on my jeans.

"You going to school like that?"

"Yes."

My parents are not strict and old-fashioned like some parents. Once in a while, my mother says she wishes I would take more of an interest in girl's things, but mostly, they leave me alone. So I am surprised by this question about my fashionably tattered jeans. I brace myself to fight to wear clothes of my own choosing. I have a right to self-expression.

"Do all the kids dress like that?"

"Yes." Not true – kids in the college-bound or art school track dress like that, but not all kids.

"How can you tell the poor kids?"

"We can't." Not true. Poor girls wear tight jeans, thick make-up and pastel colors. But somewhat true. The patched jeans crowd is easy-going and welcoming. The kids of architects and lawyers rub flannel elbows with the kids of welfare moms and factory workers, no problem. We will sort ourselves out after graduation.

True or not, I give that answer to give my father happiness. A vision of a school full of patched-pants kids, indivisible. The moneyed kids – and I know he thinks of me that way – taking on a poor kid's badge of shame, like the King of Denmark wearing a Star of David during the Nazi occupation. I am glad to give my father that vision. I am happy that my tattered jeans give us a moment's solidarity. He shakes his head, snaps the newspaper, and smiles.

Then he looks at the clock, puts aside the paper and bends to put on his heavy work shoes. He winks at me and says what he always says before he leaves for the factory.

"Off to the salt mines!"

SOMETIMES WHEN my father comes home from drinking, he is in a happy mood. Not very often, but tonight he is happy and wants me to sit with him. He even offers me a beer, though I'm only sixteen. But it doesn't feel daring or exciting to sit on the couch and drink beer with my father, the way it feels when I ride around and drink with friends on weekends.

"You're never home," he says. It's true. There's school, track and field practice, the Drama Club, and my new job. I have just come in from working as a waitress to earn money for college tuition. I don't know where I'm going to college, only that I'm going. My father encourages this, says I will be able to do anything I want with a college education. "Get that sheepskin!" he says. I have no idea what that means. I just want to leave this house and college looks like my best ticket out.

The rare times when my father talks after drinking, he never really says anything, but I'm supposed to sit and listen. He says the same things over and over. Sometimes he cries and says how much he loves his family. I wish I was brave enough then to say something like, "If you love us so much, why did you push Mom down the stairs last week?" But things like that sink below the surface of our lives together, and sometimes I wonder if they really happened. Nobody ever mentions them and I doubt my own recollection.

Tonight he tells me about the purse. It's a Depression story. I stand and listen, do not sit down. It's ten-thirty and I still have homework to do. I need to keep my grades up to earn a college scholarship.

"My buddies and I would take a purse and fill it with smelly old dog's mess. Then we'd tie a string to it and lay it down on the sidewalk. Some old lady would come along. She'd get all excited. (He widens his eyes and paddles his big hands in front of him.) She'd go to bend down and pick it up and we'd yank the string. She'd chase that purse all the way down the street and we'd be pulling the string, and she'd be chasing. . . . Then we'd stop and let her grab the purse. (He mimes opening the purse. Then the punch line.) Pee – yooo!"

He laughs in a weepy kind of way and looks disappointed when I don't laugh with him. The story always makes me feel crude and small. I don't like the story, but even if I dared, I could not tell my father why. I picture the disappointed old women. I know the story has something to do with the Depression. That money was always out of reach. But it's a cruel story. I cannot not force a laugh, though he sits waiting, expectant.

My father tells only three stories about his childhood. Two are dreary lessons, but he tells the purse story like it's hilarious. I think it's embarrassing and pathetic.

H E WANTS TO remember it as a joke.

Philip and his pal, Chet, a Polish kid with a blocky blond head, are walking down the street. They see the purse at the same time. Both boys scramble to pick it up. They shove each other. Philip puts out a leg to trip Chet. Chet falls forward, reaches, the purse is now in Chet's fingers, Philip snatches it away, fumbles it. They both lunge –

"Gimme, Rusty! I had it first!"

Philip snatches it up and curls himself around it.

"Finder's keepers!"

"But I had it first!" Chet is almost crying.

Philip crouches over the purse. It's a lady's purse, with dark shiny cloth, chipped brass jaws and a clasp like two worn fangs. Philip snaps it open. Empty. It is not stuffed with greenbacks. It's an old purse with a tiny rip in the bottom. Someone probably threw it away. They had fought over nothing.

Philip and Chet try to laugh off their disappointment. They look at the purse, not at each other, and laugh. Philip thinks of the way he tore the purse out of Chet's hand. Dirty fighting. Chet had it first, fair and square. But all he was thinking of was greenbacks, the old purse full of crisp dollar bills folded up inside. What a fool.

Chet gives one last flat laugh. Philip laughs too, ha-ha. "Joke's on us, Rusty."

Chet's not mad at him and that makes it worse. Philip thinks of how they fought like two dogs over a scrap of rotten meat. He starts to throw the purse into the street, then stops. He has an idea.

"We need a string and a piece of dog crap."

Chet sees the plan right away and pulls a piece of fishing line out of his pocket.

They lay the purse, a slight bulge in it now, in the middle of the sidewalk. Philip pays out the fishing line until they are an unsuspicious distance away. They lean against a board fence beside a big elm tree. They can spy on the purse by looking between the fence and the elm.

They shove their hands in their pockets to look casual. Chet whistles "The Beer Barrel Polka," then "The Too Fat Polka." Philip is bored already and of course, anyone is going to notice the fishing line. He is singing along with Chet's whistling – I don't want'er you can have'er she's too fat for me OH! she's too fat – and suddenly there's Mrs. Nason coming along the sidewalk with a big shopping bag. Nice Mrs. Nason, who gives his mother jars of home-made jam. Philip wants to yank the purse out of her sight but it is too late. She's seen it.

Mrs. Nason stops, looks around to see if anyone sees her, then bends awkwardly with the shopping bag in her arms. An onion falls out of the bag.

"Pull it!" Chet whispers.

Philip yanks the string and the purse skitters out of Mrs. Nason's reach. She straightens up and looks around. She knows something's up. She puts out her foot and pins the purse with her toe before Philip can yank it again. She bends down in a business-like way and grabs it. She finds the string and gives it a fierce tug. Philip gives the line lots of slack. She's going to open it, nice Mrs. Nason. Chet snickers but Philip is feeling sick. He yanks the purse one last time. But she is fast, she is determined. Money! Found money! She holds tight and opens the purse. She stands for a minute, wide-eyed, then drops the purse with a sad, outraged wail that seems to go on for a very long time.

Mrs. Nason bends down slowly to pick up the dropped onion, which has rolled toward the gutter, then leans with one hand on her knee to rise. She stands with her head down, staring into her shopping bag as if trying to figure out how she came to this moment. Philip wishes he had a green-back, so he could run down the street and give it to her. Then she raises her head. Her eyes follow the string from the purse to the tree, to the two boys behind the tree. With a wild yell she runs at them. They stand stock-still, waiting for punishment. Then Chet breaks into a run and Philip takes off after him.

They cut through back yards, then duck into the alley between the bakery and the cobbler shop and stand bent over, hands on their knees, catching their breaths. Then they begin to laugh. They laugh, hugging their ribs, hanging onto each other, laughing until tears run down their cheeks.

"Did you see her face?"

"She was so mad . . ."

As Chet said later, it was funnier than Amos 'n' Andy. He was out a good piece of fishing line, but it was worth it. Philip laughed and agreed, but on the walk home he kept his eye out for Mrs. Nason. He hoped that the next time he saw her, she would have forgotten about the purse. He hoped he would forget it, too.

I HAVE BEEN OUT riding my bike and missed Grampa Paul's visit. Now he's ready to leave. I don't care. I sneak into the kitchen to get a glass of water and hope he will leave soon. The house smells funny and I wonder if it's him or the whiskey he drinks when he's here.

"Grandma Paul was a saint," my mother tells me. She is rinsing plates at the sink from Grampa's visit. She's talking low because he and my father are still in the living room, having one last drink. I remember my father's mother as a heavy, round-faced old woman in a rocking chair. I don't remember ever hearing her speak. My mother says Grandma Paul would get up before sunrise to cook a big breakfast for my grandfather and his hunting buddies. "He never appreciated it," she says. "He didn't treat her very well." Her eyes slide away for a second and I know this means he hit her. We don't talk about that.

My mother has a deep and abiding bitterness toward my grandfather. I hardly ever see him, but I share my mother's bitterness. I have never seen anything that contradicts my mother's indictment of him. My father is evidence enough.

My father calls to us to come say goodbye and we go out

to the front steps. Grandpa Paul is standing on the cement walkway below. He is a skinny old man in a white shirt and plaid tie, a vest and a jacket. Like most old men, he is too dressed up for a hot summer day. My father is wearing slacks and a short-sleeved shirt and my mother is in pedal-pushers and a sleeveless blouse. His old man's wispy white hair is combed carefully across his bald scalp. With his sunken mouth, red wattled chin, and the big Adam's apple in his scrawny neck, he looks like a turkey.

"Look at me," he says. "Fit as a fiddle!" He does a little jig on the walkway. His shiny dress shoes clack on the cement. My father is standing next to him, waiting to get him into the car and drive him home. Since Grandma Paul died, Grandpa Paul lives with my aunt and her husband, a church-going man who keeps him in line. My mother flicks a mosquito off my bare arm. We are his un-delighted audience. But he does not see us, we could be any gathering of people. He might do this performance in a bar for drinks, or at an old friend's wake, or a meeting of the Olde Time Fiddlers' Club, where he's quite a star. I don't think he knows my name.

When my father finally gets him into the car and drives away, my mother sits down on the steps. "HIM. Fit as a fiddle. Doing his little jig. And there's his son, standing next to him, so heavy."

It's true my father is heavy – tall and beer-bellied, with meaty shoulders, puffy around the eyes. But I know my mother means something else. She sees the weight placed on him at an early age, that burlap bag of stones handed to him by the crowing, light-footed old man who danced his jubilant dance in the hot summer sun. For this my mother hated him, for giving my father the heaviness that grew each year, until he stood, slump-shouldered and tired, while his father pattered his feet on our walkway, sleek and well-cared for as a house cat.

PHILIP SENIOR WAS a lace weaver, skilled at his trade. He stood at his machine every morning. Collars for ladies' dresses, doilies for the backs of upholstered chairs, dining room curtains, all flew through his fingers. These were hard times. Most of the mills along the rivers in New England were shuttered. But oddly, in the midst of this Great Depression, there was a call for something as frivolous, as unnecessary, as lace. Further up the river, tea-colored water slid over dams, unused. But the town of Valley Few was lucky. Its mill was still producing lace.

Philip Senior was very lucky. Though the mill had cut hours and sent good men home, he stood in line at the payroll office every Friday. Every morning he went striding down Main Street on his way to the mill. See him: long legs scissoring along the sidewalk, tall and thin, erect and proud. Clean-shaven and his hair slicked back. Young-looking, despite the hair thinning across the top. He is fussy about his looks. A bit of a small-town dandy. His shirts are ironed just-so by his wife (he taught her exactly how he wanted them). His boots polished the night before by his girl, Ruby. A "bon vivant" say the French-Canadian women as he strides by, whistling one of the tunes he used to play on his fiddle at the old country dances on Saturday nights. "And his wife, so plain, like an old memé."

It was true. Where Philip Senior (never Big Phil or Old Phil, he put a quick stop to that) was boyish and friendly, Mabel was quiet, her lips tight over her teeth. She was thick-waisted after the babies and wore loose-fitting housedresses and the same old coat for years. Philip Senior was usually by himself on Main Street, sometimes with his boy or the older girl, Ruby. Mabel stayed home. If someone walked by while she was hanging clothes in the yard or shaking a rug, she'd give a quick nod to their greeting and go on with her work, hardly raising her eyes.

Mabel, when young, had fallen in love with the dark-eyed boy who played the fiddle at the country dances at the Grange. She was not a good dancer, heavy-footed and too deliberate in her movements. And she sweated. As soon as she stepped onto the dance floor, sweat sprung from her armpits and dripped down her sides, soaking her best cotton dress. She went to the dances, but stood with her back against the wall, arms folded across her breasts, and watched the tall fiddler boy with the flashing brown eyes. A big-boned young woman, her red hair frizzy in the damp heat of a summer night, wide feet crammed into her sister's old Sunday shoes. So certain was she that the fiddler boy did not see her, as she stood and watched week after week, that she was startled when he walked up to her at the break one night and handed her a cup of lemonade. Surprise saved her from tongue-tied embarrassment. So surprised was she that she just took the offered cup, smiled up into his shining eyes and gave a genuine and hearty thank you. She was thirsty.

After that night, he sometimes looked down from the platform that served as a stage and smiled a secret smile, only for her. Once, after finishing a galloping solo on his fiddle, as he stood with his head bowed to the whistling and cheering crowd, he turned slightly and gave her a wink. That wink said it was all for her. The intricate melodies, his wild slashes with the bow at the strings, the way he sometimes closed his eyes when he played a sweet ballad. All for her.

The other girls danced across the floor, whirled by their partners in time to the music, unaware of the fiddler. Only Mabel, leaning against the wall, tapping her blunt fingers against the boards, watched him all night. When the occasional awkward fellow, usually someone new to the Grange hall, came up to Mabel to mumble an invitation to dance, she shook her head no. Instead, she waited for the band to take a break, when the tall, young fiddler would lay aside his bow and wipe his face with a clean white handkerchief – not for him a shirtsleeve or collar. Then Philip would bring her a cup of lemonade and stand with her. He would take a flask from his back pocket, pour it into his own cup (the Grange, owners of the hall, frowned on liquor) and gulp it down. He tapped his feet while he drank, as if his body still kept time to the music. She found herself aware of his body, as though it was something he carried with him, something apart from him, like the half-moon riding across the big square windows of the hall. He would fetch himself another lemonade as she sipped her first, "doctor" it with a wink, and gulp it as the other young fellows in the band ambled back up onto the platform.

One night after the dance was over, Mabel waited to walk home with her friends, Lillian and Dorcas. She looked back at Philip, who was packing up his fiddle into its case. He – did he feel her eyes on him? – looked up and when she gave him a shy wave he held up one finger – Wait! – and hurried across the floor. Lillian and Dorcas exchanged a quick look of surprise. Mabel saw the look and felt an odd mixture of pride and shame. The handsome fiddler liked her. Yes, her, with her sweaty armpits and frizzy hair.

That night, they walked together with the moon high in the sky like a half-shut eye. When they reached her house, Philip leaned toward her, stumbled a little – the flask, the quick gulping – and kissed her cheek. He was forward, maybe taking advantage. Lillian had bragged about slapping a boy for doing the same. But Philip had a young sweetness about him. He seemed as surprised by the kiss as she was. Mabel was charmed by his awkwardness. Despite his height and the skill in his hands as a fiddler and a lace-weaver, Philip was a boy, eighteen to her twenty years. She was old enough to know what marriage was for – to have those long skillful fingers, that quick wink and smile, for her alone. Marriage begins with such sweetness.

I T IS A WINTER NIGHT. Or maybe late spring, when the nights are still cold and the house is damp.

Philip wakes in the midst of it. How did it start this time? The windows are closed, the town asleep. Ruby and May silent across the hall. Philip is awake, the listener, the witness. Curled like a rabbit in his blanket, ears straining in the dark. His father's voice, like a monster waking in chains, his shouts and the bitten-off silences between them. He yells and hits something, something solid, a quick rap, then his fist, his fist against a door? the table? Three things crash at once – glass, a thump, a grinding – things swept off a bedroom table? No, the kitchen counter. Good, they are in the kitchen, not the bedroom. The bedroom is less known to him. Something falls, breaks once, then lies still. A jar. Then his mother's recipe box, the whoosh of the cards across the floor. His father's shouts come faster, he is saying the same thing over and over, it rises and falls in the same cadence, though Philip cannot make out the words. Heels against wood, back and forth. Sounds rise in a rush like a brushfire up a hill. (His mother will say, not tomorrow

53

morning, that will be too soon, but she will say later, "He just flares up.") One heavy thump, something too heavy to bounce, what is that heavy? What in the kitchen is that heavy? Big and soft and heavy. But there's his mother's voice, like a breeze her voice comes up the stairs. Soft, like the way she talks to the chickens in the yard. Then a sharp yelp – what is he doing? what is he doing? A sharp, wet sound. His voice is rising higher now, there's a scrape – a chair – she is trying to get away – a low, heavy scrape – the table. She's wedged between the table and the cupboard. A thud, then the hollow sound of her body slamming against the cupboard. Again. The terrible scrape of a chair across the floor. Has she fallen, pushing the chair as she goes down? Silence. Her voice (her standing voice, thank God). They must be facing each other, the table between them. Her voice comes again, low, as if by keeping her voice low, she can make sure the sleeping children are not awakened. Then his fist – bam! – on the table. The salt and pepper shakers jump, the jelly jar, Philip's heart, his stomach.

He hates that she does not fight back.

He hates that he does not fight, that he lies still, barely breathing.

He hates that she –

He hates that he –

Crouched upstairs like a rabbit.

The thick sound of his father's breath. Tired. It's over.

His heart bangs. His blanket lies on him like a hill of sand. It is not sleep, it is an invisible weight that presses on

54

him now. He cannot make himself rise from his bed and walk down the stairs.

He hears the sound of sweeping, the straw broom shushing back and forth across the floor. Gathering all the broken things. Then the click of the salt and pepper shakers back in their places on the table. The recipe box back up on the shelf. His mother sniffs. She pushes the chair back into its place. She is so far away from him. Ruby and May are in their beds across the hall. He can no more go to them than walk to China.

It is only later, when the house is quiet. When it is all over. When Philip can finally push away the suffocating blanket. When he can finally stretch his cramped legs, blink his dry eyes. It is then he knows what he should have done, will do next time, what he always wishes he had done:

Hit him

Hit him in the face with the skillet

Back him up against the stove with the carving knife

Bash him again and again

Make him apologize

Make him promise to never do it again

Philip is wide awake now, alone in his bed, the shattered night all around him. Sweat pooled in the hollows of his knees, in the crook of his elbows. Yes, what he will do next time . . .

A train whistle blows. The world is out there in the darkness. A dog barks, once, and again. The night sounds of the world. Finally, in the small quiet house, even Philip sleeps.

I HAVE A SNAPSHOT taken on the day of my father and mother's wedding. They stand together in the back yard of a house with dark shingles, no shutters, the house my mother grew up in. Laundry hangs on a line behind them, towels and washcloths, and the grass needs cutting. As though the world had to go on, could not take the time for their wedding day.

My father is in his Navy uniform, his dress whites. One strand of the tie knotted around his sailor's collar is askew, was pulled across his chest when he put his arm around my mother to draw her closer. My mother is wearing high-heeled pumps so the difference in their heights is not as noticeable. She is in a double-breasted tailored suit, a large corsage pinned on the collar. She's wearing a brimless flowered hat that sits right on top of her head with a bit of netting sticking up. My father is hatless, his hair perfectly combed. They are looking into the sun, not smiling, long shadows behind them. It must be late in the afternoon – they look tired.

There's another photo with their parents standing behind them, my mother and father crouched in front like a team photo. No one looks happy in this photo except my mother's father, raised on a barren island off the west coast of Ireland and probably happy to be anywhere else for the rest of his life. My mother's mother looks very unhappy, though she likes her handsome new son-in-law. She did mention his drinking once, probably in that Irish way of gentling an opinion into a soft question. "You don't think he drinks a little too much, do you?" But there's a war on, everyone drinks, everyone needs to have a good time.

My father's parents look wary and sour. Maybe they are tired of being dressed up and just want to go home. My mother is crouched in front of them, in her fitted skirt and high heels. My father's mother extends her arm, steadying my mother in her awkward pose. I wonder why my mother doesn't lean on my father, who is kneeling on one knee next to her. Then I see – he is not really kneeling. His knee, in his dress whites, is not touching the ground. He's trying to keep his pants clean. He is as unsteady as she is.

There is another photo, of the women in the wedding party, the girls. My father's mother gives a tight-lipped smile from the very edge of this photo, as though she was coaxed to join in at the last minute. She looks dowdy next to the younger women, who are sharp and stylish in their well-cut suits and dresses, high heels and carefully waved hair. They stand in a row, the laundry waving behind them, an upended bench and a small metal trash can squatting in the background. My mother has one arm linked through the arm of her sullen younger sister. Her other arm is linked with my father's glamorous older sister, whose high cheek-bones and deep-set eyes gleam even in this slightly out-of-focus photo. Behind her stands my father's other sister, named for her mother, tall and lanky like her father.

I didn't know that these photos – my parents' only wedding photos – existed, until after both of my parents died. My mother always referred to it as a wartime wedding. Quick, nothing fancy. The groom in uniform, just family members to witness the ceremony. "That's how everyone did it then," she said. Once, I asked my mother if they went on a honeymoon.

"We were supposed to go to New Hampshire. But Dad got drinking – you know how he gets." She flicked her hand, dismissing the whole event. But the hurt and helpless fury were still in her voice, decades later. I never asked my father about his wedding day, though sometimes, in a sentimental mood, he called my mother his bride.

My mother's sisters are visiting from out-of-state and my cousin Noreen, a year older than me, is looking in our bathroom mirror giving me tips on how to put on make-up. I'm bored. Outside is a summer day. I tell her I don't wear make-up.

"Oh, you will," she says. "And once you start you won't go out of the house without it." She is thirteen. She smears on blush and blue eye-shadow. I look at my sunburned face and my eyes, so deep-set that no eyelid shows, and wonder what I would do with make-up.

I get her away from the mirror, doubtful she'll agree to taking a walk in the woods down to the river, but hopeful. Last time she was here, I showed her how to climb a tree. She can't have changed that much in one year. She stops to look at the photos on the wall in the hallway. The photos have always been there and I never look at them. They're dusty, and my mother gives me a dirty look as she walks by. She does not want Noreen to tell her mother, my mother's younger sister, what a poor housekeeper she is.

Noreen points to a photo of my father in his sailor uniform, when he was thin and young. His head is tilted to one side, and he smiles a confident smile. My mother, when she is not saying things about his drinking and how he never lets her do anything, says he used to look like an old time movie star.

"He was cute," Noreen says. "You look more like him than your mother."

"No I don't," I say before I even think about it.

"Well, you don't have to get all agitated," Noreen says, drawing out the last word very dramatically. "It was a compliment."

"I am not agitated. I'm just nothing like him."

I look down the hall, see my father sprawled on the couch, a drink in his hand, laughing. His face is red and his big belly strains the buttons on the new shirt he is wearing for our visitors. He's in a good mood this afternoon, the life of the party, as my mother says. His mood could change any minute, though. My mother says she'd like to have more visitors, but she can't. "Not with him around, you never know when he's going to blow up." So she only invites her sisters, who have husband troubles of their own.

"My dad didn't even send me a birthday card this year," Noreen whispers. Noreen's father left them years ago. I've never seen him. I imagine my father leaving and do not feel the pain I see under all Noreen's make-up. I think it might be a relief.

"Maybe I look like him a little," I say to agree with her, to make her feel better. "Maybe around the eyes."

Late that night, after the visitors have left and my parents are sitting in the living room, not talking to each other because of something that was said or done, I lock the bathroom door and look in the mirror. Noreen was right. I look at my eyes and high cheekbones, look down at my wide hands. I think of my father in his sailor uniform, smiling with his big white teeth. I smile at the mirror, flash big white teeth. But I am nothing like him, really. I will never drink like him, never spend my time in bars. I will not just work and sleep and watch TV like him. I will have a very different life. I don't know what it will be, but it will be different from his.

Years later, I am sitting in a bar with friends at college. We are talking about our childhoods, which seem very long ago. It's a way of telling each other, of explaining, who we are now. The talk turns to our fathers. Russell says he remembers waiting up at night to see his father when he came home from business trips, how excited he was to hear his key in the door. Alexa says her father taught her how to drive, then how to change a tire so she would never be stranded. She says he never missed one of her high school field hockey games. Mark's father is a doctor and Mark wants to follow in his footsteps. Claudine says she has inherited her sense of design from her father, an architect. Then it is my turn. I swirl the beer in my glass, thinking of my father, the endless bottles, how I spent so much of my long-ago childhood trying to avoid him.

"My father," I tell them, "made the best fried chicken in the world." I tell them that my father always encouraged me to go to college, that he had the same expectations for me as he did for my brothers. These things are true, but I feel that I have invented this father for my new college friends. My real father is hidden in the things I do not tell them. How I never saw him read anything but the local newspaper. How he loved a bargain, would paw through discount bins and treasure tables, wear shirts so cheap the cloth would squeak when it rubbed together. How he cashed his paycheck every week and spent it until it was gone. These things are more shameful, here at college, than his drinking or his violent temper.

None of my friends' fathers, wonderful though they are, can cook. Mark says his father doesn't know how to make a sandwich. Alexa says my father sounds like a man ahead of his time, like her own dad. Russell says, "I bet you miss him when you eat that dining hall chicken!"

For a moment, I do miss him. Or an image of him, smiling with a plate full of his good fried chicken. I can almost imagine that I love and admire him, this man I just invented for my college friends.

At the end of the school year, my friends are eager to go home for the summer. I feel guilty that I don't want to go home, but I cannot imagine spending the summer back at my parents' house. That is my past, a dull, gray place, and I want to stay in the bright present I have discovered away from home at college.

The only job I can find is shelving books at the college library. It doesn't pay enough for me to rent a room and still save money for tuition, so I pitch a tent in the woods behind the Athletic Complex and shower in the women's locker room. At night, I go to an off-campus bar where the local fishermen buy me drinks.

One night at the bar, in a moment of guilt and sentiment, I call home to say that I will be there for the weekend. My father answers and asks if there's anything special I want to eat. I ask if he'll make some of his famous fried chicken. He laughs and says sure. He sounds happy that I'll be home, sounds like the father I invented for my friends.

When I get home, my parents' car is not in the driveway and the house is quiet. It's eighty degrees and muggy, but all the doors and windows are shut. My mother does this when my father yells, so the neighbors won't hear. The house stinks of cigarettes and I go through the kitchen, the living room, and my old bedroom, and open the windows. I see my mother down the hall, asleep in their room, curled on her side on top of the bedspread. There's a bruise on her upper arm, or maybe it's just a shadow. I think of waking her, of asking what happened. But she will only say, as she always does, that he just flared up. She will wave away my concerns, my offers of help, my tuition money for a divorce.

I take a pack of my father's cigarettes from the kitchen drawer and sit at the kitchen table smoking. I figure I'll wait a half an hour. After twenty minutes, I open the refrigerator, looking for fried chicken, hating myself for even hoping. After a half-hour, I write my mother a note saying I didn't want to wake her, and I drive back to my tent.

I decide that I will not invent my father again. When anyone asks about him, I stare off into the distance and say we are not close. It sounds dignified and discourages questions.

I T WAS HIS FATHER that wanted to call him Philip. His mother had other names in mind. Certainly not her own father's name, that man who had run off when she was six years old. She'd never speak his name again. But she'd been whispering other names to herself, handsome ones that she enjoyed saying over and over. So when his father said, "Let's call him Philip," she chuckled and said, "What have you done so great, to name a boy after you?" She said it lightly, intending a joke. She had just given birth, she was tired. Then she saw the tears that came to his eyes before he jumped up and walked to the window, where he stood for a while tapping his fingers against the sill. There was only one way she could make amends.

Philip. A fair-skinned, red-haired boy born into economic depression and war, and a family where all that played out on a small, daily scale.

When he is born, his parents live in a room in his grandmother's boarding house. His mother's mother is a severe woman who does not like nonsense, and she finds much in the world to be nonsense. She considers it charity to rent a room to her daughter and son-in-law, though they pay the going rate. His other grandmother is a woman stunned into silence by her husband's sudden and unlooked-for death, and the creditors who came afterwards to take their farm. She is not a forgiving woman. She remembers that her son left the farm and never returned. She forgets he was only thirteen at the time.

Philip is big for his age, even as a toddler. It is late afternoon and he has just woken from a nap. His fine gingery hair stands up on his head in little peaks and his feet are bare. He and his sister share a trundle bed that gets tucked under the big bed in his family's room. But his sister refuses to take a nap, and he wakes alone in the tiny bed. The snap of clean-scrubbed sheets on the line in the back yard comes up through the open window. He slips out of the room and stands at the top of the stairs. His mother has told him he must not go poking around Grandma's house, bothering her or her boarders. But he is hungry and the smell of bread baking in the oven comes up the stairs from the kitchen. He grips the stair post and stretches out one bare foot, puts it carefully on the step below. The stairway is dark, but the square of wooden floor at the bottom shines in the light from a parlor window. One empty shoe lies on its side in the sun.

He steps down again, carefully, breathing the smell of bread deep into his empty belly. Then – shouts, scratches, clatters, a door bangs. His father's hunting dogs come pouring through the sunny square at the foot of the stairs. They are a tangle of spotted legs and whip-like tails. Their black claws and long white teeth shine in the sun.

His grandmother roars from the kitchen – "Get 'em out of here!" Then his father's voice comes light and laughing – "Come on Lucy, let's go Blackie!" The dogs tear through again, heading the other way, yelping and snapping. One dog looks up and sees him, all eyes, tongue and teeth. Philip gives a little gasp, loses his grip on the stair post and pitches forward. He feels terror, not of the hard wooden stairs, but of falling into the teeth and claws below.

Then his father is there, lifting him high above the baying, slobbering dogs. He holds him to his chest, and Philip grabs the front of his shirt, grips the rough wool in his small fists. One of his ears is pressed to his father's steady heart beat, the other is cupped by his father's warm hand. When his father speaks, his voice comes to him as a muffled, rushing sound, like water. "It's all right now . . ." Philip closes his eyes, feels himself carried along the hall to the kitchen. Outside, the dogs are still baying, hungry and wild.

His father sets him down on a bench at the table next to his sister, and goes out the door. His grandmother sets a loaf of bread on the top of the stove and cuts it into thick slices. His mother butters a slice for him and folds it to keep it warm. He and his sister sit and eat. His mother and grandmother drink hot tea though it's summer. His grandmother's boarders pass by in the hallway, tipping their hats and nodding to her on their way to the stairs. She points with her chin at the door and says, "Him. He's got money to go out and have his own good time and to feed those dogs of his. But he can't put a roof over his family's head." She is talking about his father.

His sister sets her bread aside and looks across the table at their mother, waiting. But his mother stirs her tea and says nothing. "I can't keep on with this charity, and him going out nights spending his pay." Still, his mother says nothing.

His sister sits up straight, folds her arms like a grown woman and speaks. "Pa has to go out to play his fiddle and bring me a Tootsie Roll," she says.

His grandmother laughs. "You're just like him – bold as brass." She pours more tea for his mother. "I warned you what he was like."

"No you didn't," is all his mother says.

A short time later his father moves them to a house with a fenced-in yard and what seems to Philip like many dark, empty rooms, though the house is small. He sleeps alone on a cot in a room upstairs with one window, his sister far away across the hall. The wooden rafters above his head are full of swirling faces and shapes. There are no longer the comforting sounds of his grandmother's boarders going up and down the stairs, their coughs and shuffling feet.

They do not have enough of anything to fill this house and it stays empty, though in time there are chairs and plates and an icebox, and in more time, another sister. But she is a quiet baby, and her arrival barely stirs the house. She is not enough to keep his father home at night.

Only his father can fill the empty rooms in this house, with his laughter or his fury. But he is always leaving, and his return is no guarantee of happiness. Moving to that house is the first big event in Philip's life, and because his father's shouts and silences seem to begin there, he blames the house for their troubles. He grows older and cannot remember that there ever was a time before their troubles.

One day his uncle Omer and some of his aunts and cousins are visiting and his father says to everyone, "I remember the time Philip fell down the stairs and was so scared of the dogs." He turns to Philip and says, "Remember how you were bawling like a big baby?" Everyone laughs and Philip is ashamed and furious with his father. He shakes his head and says he does not remember. But even as he says this, he feels the roughness of wool on his cheek. He remembers the flash of teeth and the howls of the hungry dogs. And something else, something like the sound of water, but this he truly cannot remember.

PHILIP'S OLDER SISTER is Ruby, named for her birth-stone, the month of hot July. A girl named for a jewel. Ruby was beautiful, with dark, deep-set eyes and thick, red-brown hair like a movie star. Ruby was smart. She brought home perfect grades. She charmed her teachers. She was two years ahead of Philip at school and when he showed up in class, his teachers would settle into disappointment that he was not like her. A smart boy, but he does not have her flashing confidence.

Ruby saved them from being a less-than-ordinary family that kept its head down and did without. Ruby. Who ran or danced, but never walked. Who wore frayed dresses lightly, the line of the old let-down hem showing, as though she would not be wearing such clothes for long. Ruby did things that Philip did not dare. She talked back, left chores undone, sang loudly in the house, and chased the chickens. She teased Pa's hounds in their kennel, holding a piece of bread dipped in bacon grease just beyond reach until they bayed with frus-tration. But at her approach, they always wagged their tails, hung their heads and nervously licked their chops, flattered to have her attention despite the anguish she caused them.

Ma put up with Ruby's defiance, though after Ruby flounced out of the house, she would stand at the window, shake her head and say, "Mark my words, that girl . . ." Just a headshake, never all the comeuppances that lay ahead for a confident, intelligent and beautiful girl. As though to say them would call them down upon Ruby, to douse the bright flame that warmed them all. She was Pa's favorite. "She's just like me," he'd say with glee and malice. Like she was something he had unleashed on the world.

"What are you going to be when you grow up, Philly?" She called him that to provoke him and he knew the best thing to do was ignore it. He was grateful that she only called him that at home.

"I don't know. I guess get a job at the mill, maybe learn to be a machinist. They make good money. Or maybe," to her he would tell his biggest dream, "be a big-league base-ball player."

She snorted. "How are you going to do that? Are you any kind of a ball player now? You should be practicing every day."

"So what are you going to be, Miss Smarty?"

"I'm getting out of this town, for starters. Go to a city. I haven't decided which one yet. Maybe New York City, maybe even Los Angeles."

"Going to be a movie star?" It was his turn to be scornful now.

"No. I'm going to be a secretary. First, in a small office. Then in a big company, for one of the bosses. That way I'll learn how to run a company."

"Why do you want to learn that?"

She rolled her eyes. "So I can run a big company, silly Philly."

It was not a plan he could snort at. Instead, he asked if she would hire him.

"Sure. You and Ma. She can be the receptionist. She would just have to sit and answer the telephone. And May . . . she can . . . Well, maybe there will be displays of our products and she can make them look nice."

It might come true, Philip thought. Ruby had a plan, and she was going to take them all with her.

But when Philip left home, Ruby was still there. With sorrow, he left her behind. Something had changed her.

Ruby is drifting. Her quick step is slow. Her face is blurred, the sharp edges gone, her wild brightness banked like a fire in the stove. Ruby is in love. Love is a place Ruby thought she would visit after she'd seen other places. But suddenly she was there. How did it all happen so fast? It is like a tree has fallen on her.

Emil Fortin is older. Twenty-four. He has a job as a mechanic and an Indian-brand motorcycle. He likes a good time. A good time is a few drinks, dancing, and spending time with her, the prettiest girl in the valley. Then he likes to ride home on his Indian, where his mother fixes him pancakes with butter and syrup because she doesn't sleep well and would just as soon be up cooking.

Emil wants to get married. Marriage looks good to him. A pretty girl lying next to him every night, breakfast on the table every morning, someone waiting for him at the end of every day. Marriage is a place softly lit and full of children's laughter. Ease, warmth, caring. It is what he remembers before his father died.

Emil Fortin is easy to love. Not very tall, but with a lean muscular build that women like. They think about touching the smooth curves of his shoulders and arms, the hard ridges of his stomach, down past his Army belt buckle, his father's from the Great War. There is something appealing in this boyish display of homage. He has a quick smile with a flash of dimple on either side, dimples under a beard so black it shines blue, though he's clean-shaven and goes to the barber every week. There is something clean and fresh about him despite the black grease around his fingernails and ground into the grain of his fingers. The black grease seems a part of him, part of the black of his close-shaven beard, his dark bright eyes and close-cut black hair. And, if you know him as Ruby knows him, the soft black hair that grows in whorls across the muscles of his chest and around the pink of his flat boy's nipples, then runs like an inviting path down his belly.

He is slightly bow-legged which gives him a rolling walk, like a cowboy or a pirate, someone not used to trudging around on everyday dirt. He's lived all his life in a skinny frame house just outside of town, but he has a way about him as if he's recently arrived and won't be staying long. He makes Ruby feel noticed in a new way. Although Emil has known her for years, has seen her running in her mother's coat to Lavoie's Bakery for day-old bread or hanging sheets in the back yard.

Emil is an only son who's always been cherished and accepts love as his due. He's never had to work for it. When he first smiled at Ruby, talked with her, listened to her plans, he began to see that she might be a girl that would be good to be around. She saw the dark eyes, the rough black beard and rolling walk and glimpsed a place she hadn't known she wanted to visit. One night, when she stood outside the old Grange hall cooling off after a fast swing number, he cupped her cheek in his hand, a small hand for a man, and said she looked pretty all sweated up. The possibilities in that remark rang in her head all week, along with the gentle feeling of his rough hand on her face.

Life didn't need a plan. Everything you wanted came to you, if you knew to not want too much. That's what Emil said. He might be right, Ruby thought. It was tempting to just rest her head against his warm chest, listen to the steady engine of his heart and forget about striving. She was tired. Only eighteen and tired already. She was angling for a job at the mill, with the women in the packing room. Mrs. Nason had promised to put in a good word for her, but nothing ever came of it. She was filling in at the beauty parlor on Fridays and Saturdays, sweeping up hair and giving shampoos. Mondays she did laundry for a doctor's family. She didn't know what she did with the rest of her days. To fill the time, she readied her outfit for the dance on Saturday night and polished her shoes. She practiced dance steps with Philip in the kitchen, the lindy hop and the foxtrot. She washed her hair with vinegar to bring out the highlights and egg whites to give it body. She polished her nails. Saturday night had become the focus of each week, a reason for living.

The money she had left to herself after giving Ma two dollars for room and board was not enough to save for a dream. How much money would it take to live alone in a new city? She did not even have enough money to live alone in the valley. She'd be twenty-five or more by the time she could save enough for a bus ticket and a suitcase, and how would she endure the years in between?

Emil Fortin was the answer to a prayer she'd never prayed. There he was every week, smiling, holding out his hand to her. The face of an angel with a five o'clock shadow. She said his name over and over to herself as she swept the floor and folded towels. She worried when her skin had a blemish, when the heels of her shoes wore down. But when she was with him, none of that mattered. Everything seemed inevitable.

Inevitable that they would ride on his motorcycle, with its leather seat, the head of an Indian brave on the fuel tank. That after a few miles of holding him, her thighs alongside his hips, they would find a place by the river, sheltered from view. A grassy place where the river was wide and smooth. The only sound, a sparrow that threw back its head and trilled joyously, over and over. Inevitable, a future planted in Ruby's young body before she'd even started her own.

Pʜɪʟɪᴘ'ꜱ ᴏᴛʜᴇʀ ꜱɪꜱᴛᴇʀ is Ma's little May, her name-sake Mabel, but she's always been May. The springtime month. Nowadays there would be a name for her strange and quiet ways. But back then, she was just May, a pale girl with blue half-circles under her eyes.

May would not eat meat off a bone or eggs with the whole yolk showing. She would not eat anything green. There was a web around May that had to be handled delicately, looked at slant-wise. The way she walked around the house on tiptoe, the way she slept on her back with her arms crossed over her chest like a dead person. How she put her shoes by her bed, just so, and if Ma came in during the night and nudged them out of place, she would spring up and set them right again. Even if Ma bent to put them back into place, she'd hear the rustle of May slipping out of bed, then the scrape of the shoes.

When Pa went into his rages, the others sat tight as if their bodies, weighted with the urge to flee, were all that kept the house from rocking off its foundations. But May would disappear, the way a deer disappears into the bushes without a sound, leaving one leaf swaying on its stem. Later they would find her in some corner of the house, with her eyes squeezed shut, hands clamped over her ears. Our little see-no-evil-hear-no-evil, Ma called her. May would open her eyes, drop her hands, and then – not seek comfort, but only run off to continue whatever she had been doing when the storm broke.

May was Ma's favorite, and Philip and Ruby accepted this as right and necessary. Pa had nothing to do with her, rarely talked to her except sometimes when he was sentimental and weepy after drinking.

"It breaks my heart," Ma said, "the way he just passes her by."

The other thing Ma said was, "I don't know what will become of her."

When she first said this, Philip, a child himself, did not see that anything ever had to become of her. She would forever be May, gliding around the house like a ballerina, humming the same tune to herself, over and over. Later, when he was older and heard what other boys said about girls, when his own body was seething, he understood that something would have to become of May.

Philip looks at May now, notices how tall she is getting. They are all sitting at the table in the kitchen with the oven going. It's Saturday and Pa is at the mill. It's warm in the kitchen, and Ma has just pulled the bread out of the oven. There's strawberry jam to go with it, a jar from Mrs. Nason.

"Don't you want to save this for an occasion?" Ruby says,

holding up the jar. She is her father's spitting image. The high cheekbones, the slightly slanted, dark-brown eyes.

"An occasion," Ma snorts. "When do we have an occasion around here?"

May licks jam off a spoon, her eyes closed with bliss. Ma slaps her lightly on the back of her hand, not the full force of her palm against the face that Philip or Ruby would get for such a thing. But Philip does not mind. May is getting bigger, older. What will become of her?

He remembers her first day of school, how he and Ruby took her to her classroom. He didn't wake with the usual first-day excitement that year. He had a bad feeling about taking May to school. But she was six years old and it was time. He remembered his own first day of school, the newness of everything, the possibilities. A tall door opening, a big room with a row of hooks on the wall and a woman telling him he must take off his jacket. The smell of food when they all unwrapped their lunches. He did not know if May was excited or not.

Philip and Ruby took May's hands and led her to school. They brought her to her classroom and stood waving goodbye as the teacher led May to a desk at the front of the room. May did not look back at them, just took her seat and folded her hands neatly on her desk. Ruby brushed her hands together and said, "That's that."

At the end of the school day, May was waiting for them in the school yard and they walked her home.

"How'd she do?" Ma asked.

"Fine," Ruby said. "She didn't cry or anything."

"She never cries," Ma said. May went to her chair and sat humming to herself, as usual. Philip noticed that Ma did not ask her how she liked her first day of school. In fact, no one said anything more about May and school.

At the end of the week, Philip was in arithmetic class copying the multiplication tables from the blackboard. The principal, Mr. Quinn, walked in, and Philip watched from under his eyelashes as he crossed the room to talk with his teacher. She looked up and called his name. He almost hoped he was in trouble, but he knew it was about May. The principal steered him out to the hallway where Ruby was waiting.

"I want to show you both something," he said. He led them along the empty hallway, their feet sounding loud as horse's hooves on the wooden floor. They stopped at May's classroom. The door was open, all the first graders sitting in neat rows, busy with something at their desks, twitching and fidgeting as small children do. All except May. She sat still as a post. Philip wondered for a minute if she was sick or dead. Then he saw her hand moving, rubbing the edge of her jaw. It was what she often did at home, but here, with the other first graders, she looked freakish. Philip felt a flash of shame, then he was angry at himself for feeling that way. She was their little May.

"That's all she does," Mr. Quinn said quietly. "Does she act that way at home?"

Philip wanted to deny it. To say that at home she was a normal little girl who played with dolls and laughed and ate bread and jam. But he thought of how she danced when Pa played the fiddle, how she spun around and around, her eyes blank and shiny. He thought of Ma saying, "What will become of our little May?"

Ruby strode across the classroom. The young teacher looked up in surprise, but Mr. Quinn made a shushing motion to her. Ruby bent down and took May's hand from her face.

"Stop that, May. Now pick up your pencil and make your letters." May looked like she did not hear. Ruby put the pencil in her hand and May sat, not looking at it. The other first graders stopped working and looked at Ruby in amazement.

"She don't do nothing," offered the little freckled boy who sat behind May.

Mr. Quinn motioned to Ruby to come back out into the hallway.

"We can't have her in the classroom," he whispered. "You'll have to tell your mother that. She's not teachable."

"Can we try talking to her?" Philip asked. "Tell her that she needs to do her schoolwork?"

Mr. Quinn sighed. "Young man, look at her. She's not normal. Maybe your mother can find a special school for her."

Philip and Ruby looked at each other, then away. They had failed.

That Monday, when Ruby and Philip got ready for school, May watched them. Still in her nightgown, she sat eating her bread while they gathered their books and lunch bags. Philip was relieved that she didn't seem to want to go back to school. But when it came time for them to leave, she pushed her chair from the table and took their hands.

"No, May. Not today," Ruby said.

"Sit down right now!" Ma said sharply. She had never spoken to her like that before. Philip saw that she was crying. Ruby pulled her hand from May's and ran across the yard and out the gate. He was left to stand alone at the door and wave goodbye to both of them. Ma stood with her hands heavy on May's shoulders as if she was trying to keep her bound to the earth. May was moving her feet, like she was dancing to some tune in her head. He would not run from them, he owed them that. He walked across the yard to the gate, turned and waved again.

PHILIP IS WAITING with Chet on the sidewalk in front of Allie Wodecki's house. It's the beginning of summer, school's finally out. Chet's glad, he hates school, says he is going to quit as soon as he can get a job in the mill. Philip says he likes school, and Chet laughs at him. Allie joins them at last, walking around from the back of his house with his head down like he's thinking. Philip knows what he's thinking about. His father was just laid off from the mill. He was one of the big shots there, he worked in the office. Some people say he wasn't laid off, he was fired because he did something not right with the books. Pa says don't go around saying that. He says the big bosses didn't want it known that the mill was failing, that Mr. Wodecki was framed. Pa uses this word proudly, tossing it off like a Chicago gangster. Philip is burning to ask Allie about it, but he knows better. Allie is a good pal. Better to pretend like none of it is happening.

Philip can't play catch today because yesterday he caught a line drive barehanded and jammed the middle finger on his right hand. He'd give anything to own a baseball glove. His finger is swollen and he can't straighten it out, so the boys walk around in the heat and Philip is bored already. Finally, Chet, the lunkhead, says to Allie, "How's your old man?"

Allie just says, "He's all right, I guess." They walk around feeling even worse. Then Philip finds a long strip of rubber, from an old tire tube or something. Chet, for once, has a good idea. He says they can make slingshots. They go into the bushes by the river and find forked sticks, perfect ones. Allie says to look out, he has seen hobos by the river, they jump off the freight trains and camp there. But they don't run into any hobos and Philip's not afraid of them anyway. They're just poor, dirty men, looking for work.

Allie takes out his pocketknife, works on his stick, then lets Chet and Philip use it. He's a regular guy, even though his father was a big shot in town. Allie's slingshot comes out the best. He's taken the time to whittle down the knots and score the handle for a better grip. They pick up stones from the edge of the river, then find old tin cans and set them up under the train trestle. There are fire rings under the trestle where hobos make camp at night. They start shooting at the cans, and it's harder than they thought it would be. Philip loses all his good river stones and has to start using clinkers from the train track. The 3:20 Boston to New Haven train goes by and they whoop and wave. The engineer looks down and blasts the whistle for them.

Allie starts getting pretty good. Soon all three of them are hitting the cans on every shot and Chet says it's time to go hunting. They walk along the tracks, and Philip is alert for anything that moves. He has his slingshot ready and keeps pulling the stone back nervously.

They see some birds, just a flock of sparrows taking a dust bath. Allie's shot goes so wide that the sparrows don't even notice and Chet fumbles and drops his stone. But Philip sees one bird, off to the side, just watching the other birds, maybe the guard bird, he thinks, and he lets go the stone. It flies true. The birds rise up and scatter in every direction, except the one he has killed, which twitches its legs and is still. Chet and Allie cheer.

"You got him!"

"Dead-eye Rusty!"

"Let's get some more stones."

Then Chet sees the look on Philip's face. "Wait, Allie. Maybe we should just stick to tin cans. Or maybe get some bottles." He's a good pal, Chet.

So they go back to the trestle, climb down and shoot some more at the tin cans. Chet promises to get bottles for tomorrow. But every time Philip hits a can, he thinks of the sparrow, its legs kicking. It just ruins it for slingshots ever again.

The weeks go by and Philip wishes school would start. There is nothing to do. Ma tells him to go find a job, but she has no idea where a boy can find work. Grown men are out of work. They spend their days sitting on the benches outside the Post Office so they're not underfoot at home. Mrs. Nason tells him to go see Mr. Corbin at the grocery store. He has bad rheumatism in the summer's damp heat and is looking for someone to help around the store. Maybe he needs a boy to clean windows or stock shelves.

Philip washes his face and hands and slicks his hair with a wet comb, making the side part straight. He presses down his cowlick with the flat of the comb. He walks to Corbin's Store, mumbling what he will say to Mr. Corbin. I'd like a job please. I need a job. Please. Do you have some work that needs doing? Hi, Mr. Corbin. I hear you need a job. No, that's not right.

He thinks of being handed his pay at the end of the week, the look on Ma's face when he hands it to her. Because that's what he'll do. He won't buy comic books or colored pencils or chewing gum. Or a pocketknife like Allie's. Or even, if he works long and hard enough, a baseball glove, smelling of new leather. Before he knows it, he's standing inside of Corbin's, his head full of the things he will not buy with his pay. He is glad to see that Mr. Wodecki is standing at the counter waiting for Mr. Corbin to come out and ring up the register, so he'll have an extra minute to think about what to say. Mr. Wodecki turns to him and says, "It's a free country, Rusty, you don't have to just stand in the doorway."

"I'm waiting for Mr. Corbin."

"Well, that's funny. So am I. Mr. Corbin is a popular fellow today." He smiles when he says this, but the smile twists. Philip sees then that there is nothing on the counter. Mr. Wodecki is there for the same reason he's there. Philip feels like he's been sucker-punched. Then he thinks, I'll work cheaper, I'm just a boy. He sees that Mr. Wodecki is thinking this, too. But Mr. Wodecki doesn't look mad that Philip might steal the job. He looks ashamed and like he's reached some bottom where he doesn't care anymore. That's scarier than if he was mad. Philip smiles, not sure what to do. Right then Mr. Corbin comes out and looks at the two of them.

Philip gives Mr. Wodecki a big wave and says, "See you around, pal!" Without thinking, he runs out the door. When he's on the street, he wonders at what he just said. He has never talked that way to a grown-up, would never dare to be that fresh.

Later, when he got home, he explained to Ma about how Mr. Wodecki beat him to the punch. She chuckled. "Al Wodecki, sweeping the floors at Corbin's. Well, he's sure come down a peg or two."

To make her chuckle again, he told her how he said "See you around, pal!" to Mr. Wodecki, just like he was a kid. But she didn't think that was funny. She said, "You've got no right to talk to him like that. Anyone can come down in the world. At least he's not too proud to do an honest day's work. There's some who would sit in a corner with a bottle, too proud to do work like that."

It was the most she had said all at once in a long time and he didn't argue. He didn't ask who would sit with a bottle and his pride. He knew who that was.

PHILIP SENIOR IS striding along Main Street on a good sunny morning, his day off from the mill. A stocky blond boy, Stan Peiczarka's son, runs past him, then stops and turns. The boy puts two fingers in his mouth and whistles, loud enough that Mrs. Lavoie across the street, wiping the windows of her bakery, looks up startled and peeved. Philip Senior does not hear a thing. Other sounds go on around him – footsteps on the sidewalk, the spluttering engine of an old farm truck – but not the boy's high-pitched whistle. He cannot lie to himself anymore. The silent whistle tells him plain and clear, some parts of his hearing are gone. He feels sick, dizzy, like he's been kicked by a horse or handed a notice from a bill collector.

He stops to catch his breath, and a woman rushing by blunders into him, apologizing and blaming at the same time. He ignores her, he needs to sit. He wants to sink down on a curbstone and wait for the dizziness to pass. But he forces his legs to start moving again and marches himself along the sidewalk to the benches outside the post office. Idlers' benches, he's always called them. He sits and fingers his ears as if the damage might be there, though he knows it is deep inside.

He has known for quite some time, in a half-dreamed, never-spoken way, that his ears have gone bad. When he plays the high and low notes on his fiddle, he knows that he is hearing them only in memory. It pains him now, to admit that he will never hear those notes again. He can remember the sound of a boy's whistle, how it arcs through the air, clean and sharp. But Stan's boy moved so quickly, had his fingers to his mouth before Philip had time to conjure up the sound and put it in his ears.

The boy runs by him again, going in the other direction now, intent on some boyish business. Philip watches him run past, carefree and unknowing. A tremendous anger flares in him. He wants to reach out and grab the boy, shake him and throw him to the ground. He knows it's not fair, knows that Stan Peiczarka's bristle-haired boy and his soundless whistle are not the cause of his failing ears, but only the proof. He knows the cause. The mill and its infernal racket. There is no remedy.

What other sounds are gone, the highs and the lows? He sits on the idlers' bench and allows this thought to rise, makes himself promise that he will consider it just this once and not keep feeling sorry for himself. There was the bass drum in the Fourth of July parade last summer, the burly drummer pounding away and Philip hearing only the sharp sound of the snare drums beside him. Every afternoon, the low thrum of the 3:20 train, that he feels deep in his chest but cannot hear. Sparrows had been silent for a long time. The tea kettle.

But every morning he still hears that mill whistle. They must have it pitched right in the exact middle. It will probably be the last sound he hears on this earth, long after he has forgotten other sounds. How much longer will he remember the sound of the notes as his fingers play them on the fiddle, and he draws the bow across the strings?

For the first time in his life, he feels old, feels things slipping away, never to return. He thinks of his own father, that mean, hard-willed old man, felled like an oak by fever. They said he died young, but he had seemed old enough to young Philip, who got the news one short week after the birth of his own son. As if, even in death, the old man had to ruin Philip's joy. He remembers his relief at leaving his father's failing farm and the winter lumber yard. Off to the mill. At the age of thirteen, no bigger dream than to spend his days working warm and dry. He had been in the mill ever since.

How much longer, these long days spent in the roar and clatter of the machines, these days that rob his body and his music? How much longer? He had not been raised to pray and this was not a prayer. To pray you have to know what you want, be willing to get down on your knees and plead for it, be ready to strike any bargain. Prayer does not even require a God, only a strong wanting. Philip Senior does not know what he wants.

How much longer? Men were being laid off from the mill every week. Playing the fiddle will never feed a family, his father had been right about that. He hears the old man's crowing laugh, loud as if he was standing right in front of him. But that sound, too, is only a memory.

IT IS THE NIGHT OF April fifteenth. I've had an after-school job since I turned sixteen in September. There was a form in my paycheck in January but it looked complicated and I didn't read it until tonight. I didn't know I had to do anything with it. I didn't know about taxes until Reggie, one of the assistant managers, said, "Jesus H Christ, you don't know that everyone has to file taxes? By tomorrow? You been living under a rock or something?"

Now I have my W-2 form and a nineteen-page Internal Revenue Service package that I have to get in the mail tonight. I feel sick to my stomach. Reggie said you can get fined or jailed for not filing taxes. In a way, I wish Reggie had never told me about income taxes. I could have spent this night in blissful ignorance instead of struggling with IRS forms. My mother says she knows nothing about taxes, my father takes care of them, he handles all the money. He goes to one of his buddies, some sort of bookkeeper, every year. I decide to wait for him to help me. He's out at the bar but will probably not be too late because he works the early shift tomorrow.

While I wait, I sit at the kitchen table and try to make sense of the forms. It's all a jumble. Taxable Wages, Withholding, Social Security Wages. I wonder why the government doesn't just send me a bill.

At 9:35, my father comes home. I hear him open the garage door, pull the car in, hear his feet on the stairs. When he walks in, I show him my tax form and ask him to help me. He sits down heavily in his chair at the head of the table and shakes his head, no.

I am stunned. I explain that I don't understand the form and that I have to mail it tonight. My throat is tight and I'm fighting the urge to cry. He hates to see me cry. I will not get any help if I cry. He is leaning down, untying his heavy work shoes, special shoes because he has bad feet from standing on the cement floor at the factory. I think maybe he didn't hear me, so when he sits up, lights a cigarette, taps it on the edge of the ashtray that is always there for him, I ask again. He says no, gives no reason.

There is nothing more I can say. I know his temper. Last week he punched a hole in the kitchen door because a roast beef was not cooked all the way through. Now he has covered the hole with a little wooden sign, the kind they sell in tourist shops. It says "I complained because I had no shoes until I met a man that had no feet." I choke back tears.

I think of my best friend telling me how her father filled out all her car insurance forms and the tears well up again, tears of self-pity this time. I scrub at my eyes and start

93

reading the form from top to bottom, slowly, matching the words on the IRS form to the words on my W-2 form. My father sits and smokes. I realize that Withholding is my money. I fill in my Taxable Wages. I do arithmetic. My father finishes his cigarette and fiddles with the little wheel on his lighter. I find my Taxes Owed on the chart at the back of the form. I subtract. I have already paid my taxes. I check my arithmetic. The government owes me money. What a relief. At 11:30 I sign the form and stand up, stretch, look in a drawer for a stamp. My father walks down the hall to go to bed.

I step out into the quiet night and walk through the sleeping neighborhood to the mailbox on Tiogue Avenue. Even though it seems that I don't owe any taxes, I want to be able to say that I mailed my form before midnight, in case the IRS ever asks.

When the envelope slips through the mailbox slot and thunks to the bottom, a huge weight lifts from me. It's like I've awakened from a nightmare. I did it. I figured out my taxes on my own. I vow that I will never again ask my father to help me with anything. From now on, I will save my paychecks, I will pay my own college tuition, I will be free of him.

I am so elated that I start running up Tiogue Avenue, which has no traffic at this late hour. I turn, running and leaping, down Princeton Street, where the houses are all closed up and dark. I feel like I can run forever, until a police car pulls up and the cop tells me to stop. He asks me why

I'm running. Somehow, this seems mixed up with my taxes and the IRS, and I wonder what I've done wrong. I feel like I'm going to cry again. I tell him I'm just running.

"At this hour?" he says. "Why?"

"Because I'm happy," I tell him. My voice cracks and my eyes start to water. I don't feel victorious anymore, just alone. But it's dark so he doesn't see my eyes, and I'm just a girl, and his radio is squawking about someone more criminal than me. I walk the rest of the way home, tired and small, wanting the whole night to be over.

PHILIP HAS FINISHED his homework. It's Thursday night and no money in the house, the week winding down. Tomorrow will be payday, and the week will break loose again like a tree uprooted in a flood. But for tonight, all's quiet.

The supper dishes are washed and put back in the cupboards. The square plum-colored rug with its border of pale yellow roses is swept clean. Ma sits in her upright rocker, darning socks, the room so quiet you can hear the click of her needle against the wooden darning egg. Pa, smoking his pipe, is sitting in the only upholstered chair, its wings so worn all the thread runs one way across the cotton stuffing, like the way he combs his thin hair across his scalp. Ma has the lamp over her shoulder, her work requires it. Pa sits in near darkness, facing the stove's steady hiss.

Ruby and Philip are at the table playing checkers. May is playing by herself. Anyone walking up the street and peering under the blue-checked curtains (Ma always pulls the curtains before she turns on a light) would see a room full of comfort and quiet cheer. The woodwork a deep cream, the chairs dark and forthright. But mostly it is the five faces, each lost in his or her own thoughts, that would make that watcher at the window wistful to be inside among them. Ma's eyes bright in the lamplight, Pa dreaming over his pipe, Ruby's lips pursed as she considers her next move, Philip all anticipation. May, with her cheek close to her beloved sock doll.

May is sitting on an old comforter in the corner, in silent play with her sock doll, its button eyes and red stitched mouth. She has a real doll, bought from a store, a Christmas gift. It is a beautiful thing, with a gleaming china head and brassy curls. An extravagance of a kind never known by Ruby or Philip, though their jealousy barely flickers. They know the doll was an attempt to buy May's attention, to lure her out of herself and into the world of little girls.

Philip remembers the morning of the gift, Ma and Pa waiting for May to show delight in the blue glass eyes that opened and closed, the perfect china ears, the tint of pink on the plump china cheeks. May had unwrapped the tissue paper, smiled uncertainly and touched the edge of the blue-flowered dress with little puffed sleeves and the stiff netting that held the skirt out straight like an umbrella. Pa stood waiting for some flicker of girlish glee, a squeal, a shriek. The doll cost more money than any toy had a right to cost. Ma sat with her arms folded. She was not one to hope. May stood up, holding the doll. She carried it upstairs and put it on a shelf above her bed in the corner. There the pretty doll stayed, blue eyes wide open, plump china legs stretched out in front of her. May continued to play with the shapeless sock doll.

Ruby triumphantly hops a kinger back and forth across the checkerboard and Philip has lost. Fair enough, but no, he doesn't feel like another game. He hates to lose and hates that losing bothers him so much. He takes up his history book, leaving Ruby a restless winner. Ruby stands and holds her hands to the stove. It's something to do – it is warm in the kitchen, almost stuffy. Certainly her hands are not cold.

"What was it like, Pa, when you were a little boy? Did you ride horses?"

Because it is Ruby, Pa takes the pipe out of his mouth and settles deeper into his chair, his present time, and reaches back into his past. Back to times that were colder and harder, he wants his children to know, than anything they can imagine in the comfort of town-living in the 1930s.

"Horses? I drove a horse and sledge all winter. Hauled firewood and timber. Started when I was ten. Before that, I shoveled the sawdust and chips in the lumber yard and before that peeled potatoes in the camp kitchen, a twenty-pound bag a day."

"Did you name the horses?" There is a streak of the romantic in Ruby, she is not interested in potatoes.

"I didn't think much about them. I never had to call them anything. They knew the way, just down the road, down to the lumber yard. There wasn't much of anywhere else for them to go. I mostly thought about suppertime and how was I going to get my feet warm. And dry. Cold in winter and mud in spring. Six days a week and sometimes Sunday."

"Every single day?"

Pa nodded, yes.

"Then when did you go to school?"

Pa's face went tight. His lips thinned, his eyes narrowed, the curves by the sides of his nose seemed to deepen. A wind shift in the cozy room. Philip felt it. Ma looked up from her darning. Even May stopped her soft chatter to her sock doll for a moment. But Ruby didn't see or chose not to see. She was the only one among them who did not step carefully around him. Sometimes it seemed to Philip that she enjoyed provoking him. Pa shifted in his chair, hitched up his shoulder.

"On and off." He stood, stamped his feet like a restless horse himself. "That's how come my feet are always cold. Too much cold when I was young."

Philip felt sad for that boy, his Pa years ago. His cold feet, the dreary winter days spent riding a log sledge back and forth with only the nameless horses, who at least had each other for companionship.

Pa said, without looking at him, "Now Philip over there, he wouldn't have lasted a day in a lumber camp. Sitting nice and warm by the stove with a book." He spat the last word like it might sizzle against the stove.

Philip kept his eyes on his history book. They seemed to stick on one sentence and he read the words over and over: *A splattering of shots at Lexington swelled into volleys at Concord's rude bridge.* Again and again until the words made no sense. *asplatteringofshotsatlexingtonswelledintovolleys at concordsrudebridge* A thought came to him. This is what it must be like when you don't know how to read.

Philip looked up at Pa, saw Ruby looking, too. Saw on Pa's face that he knew his son and daughter had just put together that he had never learned how to read and write.

Pa stood up and set his pipe on the table. Philip cringed. Certainly there would be punishment for this knowledge. Certainly Pa would need to even the score, to prove that book-reading couldn't stop your nose from bleeding. The stove smoked and Ruby coughed and fanned her hands, trying to draw the attention to herself, draw Pa's rising wrath. Pa was already striding across the room, his boot heels booming in the quiet. But all he did was take his jacket from its hook by the door and put it on. Ma looked up from her darning with mild surprise, but he came and went as he pleased, she knew that. She went back to her work and he said nothing. He had no money for drink, and Philip wondered where he would go. He just seemed eager to get out of their sight.

Philip watched him button his jacket, bend to tie his boot lace. The old illiterate. A surge of power went through him. The old man didn't even know how to read. But just as quickly, he felt empty, with an aftertaste of shame. Ruby watched Pa, too, as he banged out the door without a backward look. She folded her arms and pressed her lips together. Philip felt his own lips do the same. They looked at each other without speaking. Ma went on darning. May had slipped off to bed without anyone's notice. Ruby said nothing, turned and walked upstairs. Ma put aside her work and stood to stretch.

"Don't forget to turn that lamp off," she said.

Philip sat for a while, his arms tight across his chest. The room had gone cold. Philip had seen Pa sign his name once, a big flourishing scrawl. But he could not read, Philip knew now, knew why he had never seen him with a book or even a newspaper. Philip would always best him at this. But it only made him feel smaller and meaner. His father's failings and weaknesses did not bolster him, they weighed on his wide, bony shoulders.

I WAKE UP, EXCITED because it's Saturday, then I hear the rain, the swish of wet tires as a car goes by. I tell myself I don't care, there will be tomorrow to spend outside in the woods, and after school on Monday, and the next day and the next.

Smells of coffee and toast are in the hallway. In the kitchen, my parents are not speaking. I heard them last night, they woke me. It seems like a bad dream now, in the kitchen with the light on over the table, our boots lined up by the back door. But the evidence is there in their silence, in the nervous way my mother scrubs at the sink.

I pour a bowl of cereal, join my brothers at the table. We try to talk normally, but it is hard. Our voices squeak, or boom out like we're in church or the library. But those are places of quiet and houses are not. So my brothers and I do our part to make this a house. We squabble over who gets to read the back of the cereal box, we hum and swing our legs under the table. When my father shifts in his chair, we freeze for half a breath, then resume our humming and swinging. My mother keeps busy, putting away the butter even though we're not through using it, folding the empty milk carton into a tight packet before throwing it in the wastebasket.

My oldest brother stands up, says he's going to go play basketball. My mother says, "It's pouring out there," but he's already gone. My father stubs out his cigarette, puts his wallet in his back pocket and goes out the door. No one says anything. But our legs swing more easily, our humming finds a tune. My brother cuts something off the back of the cereal box, he's always sending away for things. Special offer! Mail today!

It rains all morning. I sit in the living room reading a book called *The Woods for Sam,* about a boy my age who goes to live all by himself in the woods. His parents send him off with sandwiches and cookies but after he eats them, he has to forage for wild foods. At night he sleeps in a hollow tree. I want to be Sam, but the woods behind our house are hemmed in by houses, full of old bike tires and scrap lumber. Also, the book does not explain things, like how Sam would stay dry on a day like today. I am trying to learn from this book, but I'm not even sure if it's a true story. I wonder how my parents would feel if I told them I was going to go live in the woods, that I can't stand my father roaring at night, the nervous silence in the morning.

In the kitchen, my brother says, "Where did Dad go?" and my mother says, "You know where he went," which means he's out drinking. My brother wanders into the living room, asks if I want to play chess. I don't really want to play chess, but if I stop reading, my book will last longer, I can

go live in the woods with Sam for another day. My oldest
brother knows how to play chess and is in the Chess Club at
school. But my other brother and I just knock off each
other's pieces until one of us, usually me, is out of pieces. We
say Checkmate when we knock off a king, then carry on,
knocking off whatever is left. My favorite pieces are the
horse-heads. I try to protect them.

Some days I lose right away, but today the game goes
on and on. I am being crafty, thinking out my moves like
Sam in the woods figuring out how to store acorns or start
a fire with wet wood. I even knock off my brother's queen,
no one's favorite piece, but the most useful in knocking off
other pieces. I'm crowing and he's pretending to cry when
the car pulls up in the driveway. The engine roars, the tires
squeal. We stop laughing and crying. Then we start again,
but we're both pretending now, he's pretending to fake cry
and I'm pretending to laugh at him. Our ears are tuned to
the driveway, waiting for the sound of the car door, my
father's progress into the house. My brother moves a bishop.
I move a pawn, wondering why the car door has not
opened and shut. My brother reaches for his bishop again
and I see that I've left one of my horse-heads open to being
knocked off.

My brother leaves his hand on the bishop, looks up at the
window. We're sitting on the rug, so we can't see outside. It's
okay to glance up at the window, but to stand and look out
would be to admit that something is going on in the driveway. My mother is going back and forth with the laundry

basket. She is not looking out the window. She looks in at us, to make sure we are not looking out the window.

"I'll let you keep your knight just this once," my brother says. He does this to be kind, but also because the air has gone out of this game. He doesn't care about winning anymore and neither do I. But something keeps us there, moving the pieces around, taking our turns, knocking off pieces in a business-like way. He knocks off my queen and I groan, because I have to, the queen is the most valuable piece. It's like we're not playing chess anymore, we're only acting like we're playing chess.

My mother is still going back and forth with towels, stacks of sheets, the vacuum cleaner. She will not look out the window. Finally, the car door clicks open. I pretend my leg is asleep and stand up, making a show of slapping my leg and stamping it. I look out the window. My father is slumped down in the car, one leg out the door in the rain. Everyone can see this, can see he is too drunk to get out of the car. I hope my mother does not see this. My brother stands up and looks, too.

My mother stops in the doorway of the living room. Her mouth is a thin, straight line. My brother says, "What's the matter with Dad?" and she turns on him, her bottom teeth showing like a small, mean animal.

"You know what's the matter with him," she hisses, as though all the neighbors are listening. He has crossed some line, pretending he does not know why my father cannot get himself out of the car, why he's half-lying on the front seat with his pant-leg out in the rain. The thing is to pretend that none of this is happening at all. My mother stalks down the hallway.

I sit back down and tell him it's his turn. He asks if I still want to play. I tell him yes, I want to finish the game.

"You just don't want to lose," I say, which I know isn't true. Neither of us cares now. But it sounds like a normal thing to say, what a sister says to a big brother, even though it's clear that it is me who is going to lose. My queen is gone and my brother can't keep letting me keep my horse-heads without admitting that he doesn't care about winning or losing.

Outside, the car door shuts, we both jump. I reach out, run my bishop across the board, knock off a pawn. My brother moves a rook, exposes another pawn. We do not talk, we are listening. I take his pawn. We hear my father fumbling at the back door.

"Game's over," my brother says. We both still have pieces left, but I don't argue. He sweeps the board clean and heads for his room. My father is in the kitchen now, banging into things. I take off down the hall and realize, too late, that I've left Sam and the woods out in the living room. Instead of reading, I sit on my bed and make plans for the day I will leave this house and live by myself in the woods.

PHILIP HATES FRIDAYS. Friday is payday at the mill and Pa always comes home late. Though the later he is, the better. Early means something spoiled his fun at the bar and he's looking for a fight the minute he opens the door. Tonight, though, he's good and late.

Ma watches the clock on the shelf as though it's going to tell her when to serve supper. The soup's on the stove, bubbling away while they all sit and wait, hungry. Philip wishes she would just make a plate for Pa and keep it hot on the stove. That's what Chet's mother does. Chet's father is a happy, easy-going fellow, who plays polkas on a little squeezebox when he comes home after drinking. Pa wouldn't stand for a plate of food drying on the stove. He likes his meals hot and fresh.

They all wait. Philip and Ruby sit at the kitchen table. He is working on math problems. She is hemming a skirt. May walks around the kitchen squeezing between the chairs and the wall, around and around. Ma just sits, her eyes on the clock. Philip does not know how she can just sit with her hands in her lap the way she does.

Philip waits, listening for Pa's heavy foot on the door-step. Impatient and dreading it at the same time. The gate clicks. The four of them jump. May slinks down into her corner and picks up her sock doll. Pa's steps stutter on the walkway. The door swings open, he lurches in. The night's cold air comes in with him. He's loose on his legs, chuckling to himself, his jacket hanging open.

They all look at him. "Hi, Pa."

He mutters something and falls into his chair at the table. The chair teeters on two legs. They hold their breath until the chair clunks down, solid, on four feet again. Ma hurries to set out spoons and plates. Pa picks up his spoon, drops it, laughs out loud.

"Company coming! Ain't that what it means? When you drop a spoon? Wonder who's coming?" He laughs some more and half falls out of his chair as he leans down to pick up the spoon. Ma ladles soup onto their plates while Pa fumbles with his spoon, laughing and spluttering. He sits for a minute with his head bent over his plate. Philip can see the thin hair across his red, blotchy scalp. The blood must have rushed into it when he bent down. The thought makes Philip feel a little faint and sick.

They all – Ma, Philip, Ruby and May – spoon soup into their mouths and try not to look at Pa, just eat what's in front of them. Pa puts his spoon down. It clanks and they jump.

"What's the matter with all of you? Looks like a funeral around here."

They all swallow, look at each other, back at him.

"Philip!" Philip's spoon clangs against his plate. "Smile a little, son! Pretty soon, we're going to have a chicken in every pot! That's what he promised, right?"

No answer from the table. Pa looks at each of them, eyes shiny and hard. He picks up his butter knife and grips the handle.

"Well didn't he?"

"Who, Pa?" Ruby says it lightly.

"Hoover. That's who. That son-of-a-gun. Give me the butter."

He bends his wavery attention to the task of buttering his bread. They breathe again, eat. Pa sits up straight, sets his bread on the table, buttered side down. They pretend not to see.

He fixes his eye on May, his head slightly cocked like a rooster. She picks up her bread, bites and chews, keeping her eyes on his face.

"You been a good girl this week?"

She nods yes, still chewing.

"You help your mother in the kitchen?" Her jaws stop. May does little in the kitchen except sit in her corner with her sock doll. But she nods again, yes.

He shifts in his chair and digs deep into his pants pocket. He almost falls out of the chair. They hold their breath.

"Here." He holds out a dime to May. "Buy yourself a new dolly." She stares at him over the half-eaten slice of bread in her hands. He sets the dime in front of her plate with a flourish, like it's a rabbit he's just pulled out of a hat. He beams down at her in a fond, hazy way, as though she is a little stranger come to supper.

"What do you say, May?" Ruby wants to keep things moving along. Trouble starts when things stall. Ma's head is bent down over her plate. It is best when she stays out of it. Philip is not sure where he should look.

May blinks once, twice. Pa's bleary gaze is beginning to harden. Ruby mouths th-ank you-u, her lips stretching out the words.

"Thank you," May says, without turning her eyes from Ruby's fascinating mouth. She picks up the dime. She usually gets a nickel. Philip wonders if she knows the difference. Satisfied, Pa digs another dime out of his pocket. He rises slowly, like he's facing a strong wind, and hands the dime across the table to Ruby.

"Thank you, Pa."

He looks at Ruby, wanting more, miffed that she puts the dime neatly into the pocket of her skirt without even looking at it. She returns to her soup. Some weeks, when she's in a truly happy mood, she will lean over and kiss him on the cheek.

"What are you going to buy with it? Better not be lipstick." He grins at her. His teeth and gums shine like raw eggs. Ruby doesn't look up. She only says –

"Don't worry. I save my money."

Drunk though he is, Pa catches the rebuke. But he decides to eat his bread. He is no match for her. He picks up the bread and discovers the buttery mess by his plate. Ma has been waiting for this and hands him a dishrag from the stove behind her. He swabs at the table and gets butter on his sleeve. He turns in his chair and fires the dishrag into the sink, a direct hit. They jump. He eats his bread and butter. They bend their heads to their plates, grateful that he is, at last, busy with his meal.

For a while, they are a family eating supper. Ma ladles more soup onto Philip's plate. May finishes her bread. Ruby shakes salt into her soup. Ma watches her and doesn't say, though it's in her defeated look, not salty enough, not good enough for you?

Pa returns to Ruby like a hunting dog on a scent. "I better not catch you hanging around Main Street looking for boys."

"I don't."

"You better come right home. I better not catch you." He's grinning again. He'd like to catch her, Philip thinks.

"I do."

"You do what?" Pa looks genuinely confused. He's lost the thread of this talk. He's more drunk than usual, Philip realizes.

"I come right home," Ruby snaps. They all stiffen. Nobody, not even Ruby, snaps at Pa. Especially when he's like this. He looks around the table.

"What's everybody looking so gloomy for? It's payday, for jeeper's sake." Philip twitches a little smile. May gives him all her teeth. Ruby stuffs her mouth with bread. Ma is busy worrying a piece of potato around her plate with her spoon.

Philip looks at a spot on the table in front of his plate. There's a crescent-shaped dent there, as though a giant pressed his thumbnail into the wood. Philip counts five grains of salt, one stuck down in the dent.

"What are you looking so peeved about, son?" Finally, Philip thinks. It's almost a relief. "You got a hair across your behind?" Pa snickers.

Philip makes himself swallow his soup. He wishes Ma had not given him more, it's a big messy pile on his plate now. A hair across his behind. It doesn't even make sense. What a thing to say in front of his sisters. In front of Ma, even.

Pa takes a coin out of his pocket. A quarter. Oh, he is determined to get some glory this week.

"This ought to make you smile." Pa holds out the quarter, makes Philip reach across the table to take it. "Let's see you smile." Pa isn't smiling.

Philip tightens his cheek muscles, feels the corners of his mouth curl. He hopes it looks like a smile. He looks back down at the giant's thumb mark. Pa slaps his hand down on the table. The grains of salt jump. The one stuck down in the dent leaps free.

"That's all I get for a quarter?" he yells. There is soup dribbling from the corners of his mouth – good Lord, he's drunk – but Philip knows he must not laugh. He cannot imagine what would happen if he laughed right now.

"You know how hard I worked for that quarter?" Pa bellows.

A soft choking noise comes from May. Ma looks up at her and makes a motion with her chin from May's plate to the sink. May takes her plate to the counter and leaves the room. She left soup on her plate, but Pa does not demand that she come back and eat it. He never yells at May, she scares too easily. Philip watches her go. His own plate is still half full.

Ruby pushes her chair away from the table and starts to stand. Philip wants to cheer. They might get out of this after all. But no –

"So. I'm going to eat supper all by myself?" Pa lowers his head. "Nobody wants to eat with the old man." Again, Philip sees the thin strands of his hair, the shiny red skin beneath. Philip hopes he is not crying. Some weeks he cries and that is the worst. Pa's head snaps up –

"I put the food on the table . . ." He slaps the table again and Philip sees the grains of salt jump. " . . . and nobody wants to eat with me!" Pa picks up his soup plate with both hands. He looks like he wants to tear it in two. He crashes it down on the table. Soup flies up into the air, seems to hang there for a moment, then splatters down, a sickening sound. The good soup, Ma's good soup, splatters all over the table, the salt shaker, the wall. Soup is dribbling down Ma's face. Philip looks away. It's all he can do for her, to not look at her good soup dripping down her face.

Ruby is frozen, still half out of her chair. Everything is moving so slowly, Philip thinks. Why can't it hurry and be over? Ruby looks guilty. She caused it this time.

Pa hauls himself to his feet, knocking his chair backwards. The chair trips him as he steps away from the table. He gives it a savage kick. Again, Philip tries to imagine what it would be like to be able to laugh. Pa lurches over to the sink, picks up the dishrag and wipes at the soup that splashed on his shirt. Then he throws the dishrag at Ma. She makes a sound in her throat, a squeak like a rabbit in a hound's jaws. Philip wants her to throw it back at him, but that's unimaginable, like laughing.

"Go ahead – eat by yourselves!" Pa grabs his jacket, flails one arm into it and hurls himself out the door. The door hangs open into the night. The gate bangs.

Ruby finishes getting up from the table – it seems to Philip she has been half-crouched in her chair for hours – and goes to shut the door. They all breathe out heavily, as though something's been holding their heads under water.

Ma takes the dishrag, wipes her face, then wipes the table. May has come back and watches from the kitchen doorway.

"Finish up," Ma tells her and points her chin to May's plate. But they know May will not eat again tonight.

Philip takes his quarter and sets it on the counter. Friday night. Ruby stacks her dime on his quarter.

"Here, Ma."

May steps up and eagerly adds her dime to the stack, like she's making a kinger in a game of checkers.

Ma pockets the change. It's more than most weeks, but she doesn't count it. She does not look at them. She sits down heavily in her chair by the stove.

Ruby clears the plates from the table. "Maybe you can buy yourself a new pair of stockings this week, Ma."

Ma turns to look at her. Philip sees the blame in her eyes and wants to say that it's not Ruby's fault.

"I need a new washtub. The old one's rusted right through."

Philip wants to say to heck with a washtub. But it's her money. If she wants to buy a washtub, that's up to her. It was good of Ruby, though, to mention the stockings. Philip wishes Ma would thank her for that. Just smile, he thinks, and say thank you.

M Y FATHER ANNOUNCES that we are going to have a picnic at Arcadia State Park, one of my favorite places. He has made his wonderful fried chicken and chilled two cans of Campbell's beans. We have potato chips and root beer, treats we get only on special occasions because my mother doesn't think junk food should be eaten every day. My father packs the big cooler with chicken and potato salad, beer for my parents and soda for the kids. It's late August, and the air already feels like autumn. I pack a sweatshirt and a bathing suit, so I'm ready for anything.

The ride to Arcadia seems to take a long time. My father drives past all the new housing developments, "plats" we call them, full of families who've left the city and its problems. We leave our plat, which still has woods left, though more trees get bulldozed every day. I am afraid that someday I will come home from school and find bulldozers in the woods behind our house. But so far, we are lucky. We go by an older plat where the houses sit side-by-side from one end to the other, the woods long gone. Then there's the rich people's plat, Woodland Estates, where our dentist and the man who owns the local Ford dealership live. We pass

Buffalo Bob's Burger Barn and the Ford place. My father says the man who owns the Ford place is a regular guy, even though he's a big shot.

Then the highway narrows and there are trees and a gas station once in a while, with a general store. The street names change from the theme names of plats (ours has college names, Woodland Estates has trees) to funny names like Tunk Hill Road and Poor Farm Road. Finally we reach Arcadia, with its picnic tables under the pines, gravel roads and foot trails, a pond with a sandy beach. There are hardly any other families there because it's not a beach day, and the park ranger tells my father he can take any site he wants. He chooses a site next to the pond. "We can look at the water," he says to my mother.

He tells us we can go play but be back in time for lunch. My brothers take their football out to the field near the beach. My parents settle into folding beach chairs facing the pond. I put on my sweatshirt and roam around, walking the trails through the woods. I love the deep woods in Arcadia.

I walk by the stream and watch a clump of black water bugs swim in crazy circles. The swamp maples are already turning red and I pick up a few perfect leaves to give to my mother. I hop on stones in the stream and get my sneakers wet. The stream empties into a little wetland with cattails and a muddy path. I hear a loud buzzing noise and trace it to a big cicada clinging to a birch leaf. I find a turtle, a kind I have never seen before. It's small and its bottom shell, that I know is called a plastron, is smaller than the palm of my hand. When I pick up the turtle, it does not retreat into its shell, instead darts its head out and squirms to look up at me. It's a fighter. I give up any thoughts of taking it home and put it back in the water, where it dives and disappears.

The sun is high and hot and I take off my sweatshirt, think about the beach. Then I remember lunch. I run all the way back to our picnic site. My brothers are already there, eating all the chips. The fried chicken is piled on paper plates, ready to eat. My father opens a can of beans, dumps it into a bowl and says to me, kidding, "You're getting nothing but beans for lunch." My mother says, smiling, "Look at those sneakers, where did you find all that mud?" I tell her about picking up the turtle and she says it's good I let it go, everything likes to be free. My father says to go to the pond and give my hands a good washing.

We eat. A breeze kicks up over the pond and makes a fluttery sound in the pines. Clouds coast in, but we stay, finishing the fried chicken and potato salad. Finally, my father packs everything back into the cooler. He gives the trash to my brothers and lets them burn it in the stone fire pit. My mother brushes crumbs off the table with a pine branch. I sit on a rock with my chin on my knees, watching the wind ruffle the pond. I hear my father chuckle and say to my mother, "Look at her, like a little wild Indian." Then it's time to get in the car and go home.

THE SUMMER BEFORE I left for college, my father did what seemed to me a remarkable thing. He planted a vegetable garden. I had never even seen him pick up a shovel. He had never shown any interest in growing things, so I don't know when he learned to plant a garden. He did it suddenly, the way he tended to do things. Not for him the browsing of seed catalogs on winter nights. No, his garden was thrown down in a day. A patch of back yard lawn dug up and seeds planted in rows. Tomatoes, string beans, cucumbers, lettuce.

He planted the seeds and they sprouted. It was a warm and sunny June, then a hot July. By August, there were vegetables. Vegetables grown by my father, who had never spent so much as an afternoon in the back yard for the all the years we had lived in that house. Big shaggy tomato bushes, heavy with green fruit, six-inch cukes with little spines like whiskers, loose heads of lettuce. Long, well-formed string beans hanging one after the other.

I was not home much that summer. I was busy with a summer job at an ice cream stand and hanging out with friends, that clinging time before we would all go our separate ways. I did not know how or if my father cared for his garden. I never saw him weeding or hoeing. Only watering, standing outside in the quiet hour after dinner, in the Bermuda shorts he had taken to wearing and a neatly pressed sport shirt. He wore glasses all the time by then, and a big wristwatch with an expandable stainless steel band, a gift from my brothers, the only watch he ever owned.

He and my mother went away for a week that August, to my aunt's summer house in New Hampshire. The vegetables in my father's garden were just becoming ripe. "Eat them up," he said. "They'll just go to waste. Eat as much as you want."

I was home alone for the first time in my life. My parents never went anywhere. My brothers had gone away to college and not returned. I used my freedom to stay out late, to go skinny-dipping in country ponds and ride around drinking cheap strawberry wine after the ice cream stand closed for the night. I came home at two in the morning, slept a muzzy sleep until it was time to get up, shower, throw on my clothes and start all over again. I lived on wine and peach melba ice cream.

The garden seemed to ripen all at once that week. I could see big red tomatoes from the bathroom window when I dried my hair in the morning. I kept meaning to go outside and pick them. The string beans hung in fat curves, the lettuces opened and over-spilled. Every night I promised myself I would get up early in the morning and pick vegetables. I would make a meal of them, cut up a salad, boil the beans. Every morning I rolled out of bed, ran to work, rode around with my friends listening to Janis Joplin and Jimi Hendrix, then late nights of naked swimming and wine.

One day slid into the next and then it was the night before my parents returned home. I went to bed at three in the morning, my hair damp with pond water. An hour or so later I woke to thunder and watched lightning turn the sky silver-white. It poured until sunrise. When the rain stopped, I pulled on shorts and a tee-shirt and walked out to the back yard in my bare feet with a big plastic bowl. My head hurt from too much sweet wine and my mouth was sticky and sour. The clouds cleared quickly and bright sun glittered on beads of water on every leaf in the garden. It made my eyes hurt.

The heavy rain had pummeled the tomato plants. The ripe ones were on the ground, split open, seeds leaking into the mud. The string beans, seen close up, were full of big seeds. I snapped one in half and the long woody string down the side was too tough to break. I pulled them off the vine anyway, and each time I jerked one free, my brain seemed to bang inside my skull. The lettuces were crammed with dirt, the outer leaves ragged and torn. I pulled a few cucumbers off the drooping vines and found a couple of tomatoes that looked salvageable. I left the row of muddy lettuces. They were beyond me. Vegetables came out of the fridge, clean and tidy in cellophane wrappers. I had no idea what to do with all this muddy food. I left the bowl in the garage, intending to wash everything after I took a shower and got dressed for work. But then I was late and forgot about it.

I went straight home from work that night. Freedom time was over. My parents were back, their little pea-green Dodge in the driveway. My father asked about the garden. It was so easy to lie, to say I had been eating salads, to say it had been hard to keep up with it all. It was too hard to say that he had done something beautiful, and I had let it go to ruin.

He never planted another garden, and sometimes it seems as though that one never happened. But I do remember it. I see him standing alone at dusk, cigarette in one hand, the garden hose in the other. The garden thriving on that bit of attention each day, that deep soaking before dark.

YEARS AFTER my father died, I was going through a shoebox full of old papers, looking for documents my mother needed to claim his Navy pension. I opened a torn, unmarked manila envelope. Inside was a high school diploma with my father's name on it, earned when he was in the Navy. I would not have been more shocked if I had come across a love letter from a woman who was not my mother. It changed my entire view of my father. He had always been a stranger to me, but now he was a different stranger.

He had never mentioned a diploma, had always claimed, "I got no education," the bad grammar deliberate and taunting. His diploma, earned on shipboard, must have seemed second-rate to him, an imitation. He remained, in his own eyes, his own words, an "uneducated man." I had always accepted that. Now, years later, he was a man with some education. Would that have changed anything?

If he was ashamed of his shipboard diploma, he was determined that I would have the real thing, and more, that I would go to college. He liked that quip attributed to Mark Twain, "Never let your schooling get in the way of your education," but he said it with a belligerence that flaunted rather than hid his sour grapes. I used to wonder if he even knew he was quoting Twain. The one thing he did say honestly about education, that he said clearly, consistently and often, was "Go to college, get that sheepskin." He was determined that his children would become educated people, even if it meant holding his life up to us as what would happen if we did not.

I got no education, he told us. (And look at me.)

When I was about ten years old, I came home from school one afternoon and he was sitting at the kitchen table with a pencil and a pad of paper. He said he wanted to show me something. I was eager to get out of my school clothes and go outside, but he had never done anything like this before, something so fatherly. So I stopped and stood by him. He proceeded to show me the Trick of Nines. He drew a grid on the pad and showed how the digits of the multiples of nine each add up to nine. I was disappointed. I'd seen the trick before, kids at school had passed it around. But I pretended interest and surprise. I did not want to spoil his delight in teaching me something. I stood there and wished he could genuinely teach me something I didn't already know, but I didn't think there was anything. I believed in the man he held up to me, the man with no education.

By the time I was in high school, it seemed that my father and I lived in two different worlds. And, with his encouragement, I was working hard to get even further away from him. I wanted to be free of him, and I wanted, as he wanted, for me to go further in life than he had ever thought of going. We watched each other across a long distance. I avoided him, rushed by him as he sat at the kitchen table waiting to go to work. I did not invite my friends in when he was home, let them wait out front in the car.

He seemed proud of my accomplishments. He attended all my school events, sometimes traded work shifts so that he could be there. The Rhode Island Honor Society Tea, my supporting role in the Senior Play, my graduation. I took for granted that he attended these events, that he had little to do besides go to work and that these events were fun for him. To spend a Sunday afternoon in the high school cafeteria watching me receive a tiny Rhode Island Honor Society pin. He did these things when he could and I did not pay much attention to him. Had he been a peaceable man, he might have scarcely been a presence in my life. Or maybe he would have been more of a presence, an ordinary and approachable father, the father of the Trick of Nines.

I am not sure if this ever happened, or if I have run the scene over and over in my head so many times that it has taken on reality. I see myself at a high school event, some celebration, maybe the Rhode Island Honor Society Tea. The ceremony is over and everyone is milling around. I am wearing a long orange and yellow print dress and my hair is brushed out bright and shining. I stand holding the program for the event, receiving congratulations from friends and teachers.

My father is standing on the other side of the room. He is wearing a navy blue suit and is, as always, perfectly groomed. His hair is shining and neatly parted, combed back from its handsome widow's peak. His face is well-scrubbed and ruddy above the white shirt and striped tie. I know he smells like soap and sweet cologne. He is looking for me and despite his height, his girth, he looks small and lost. I yell to him – Dad! – and wave the program to get his attention. Across the room, before all the assembled people – my college-educated teachers, my college-bound friends and their parents – I claim him. Claim him with pride.

I hope I did that. I hope he looked out across that room, so crowded with educated people, him nervous and eager to get out of his uncomfortable suit and tie. I hope that when he searched for me and finally found me, he saw the pride on my bright face, saw the easy way I claimed him. I hope that happened.

PHILIP WAS A SMART BOY in a fading mill town. He and Celeste Lavoie were the smartest in their class, everyone knew it. It seemed strange to him to compete with a girl, stranger yet to have to work at beating her. But that's how it was between them. Mr. Auger would distribute a stack of algebra tests: "And the highest grade is a 96 –" Philip and Celeste's eyes would meet across the room, across the rows of students who simply waited to collect their tests, who knew they had no part in the honorifics. "– Celeste, well done." Philip gave her a thumbs-up and a tight smile. He hated to lose. "Philip, 94. Good job." He had lost again.

But no one, including him, begrudged Celeste her high marks. There was not a girl in the class who would have traded her B+ or C for Celeste's beak of a nose, her sallow skin and brown hair pulled back in a tight, no-nonsense ponytail. Celeste lacked that sense of being on view that pretty girls possess. A pretty girl like dark-eyed Marie Tate or blonde Lorraine Nelson would know enough to pull her sweater down neatly in the back before walking up to the front of the class. A pretty girl would not choose that moment, standing before the entire class to collect her top-notch test, to pull and scratch at her ear lobe. She did not flout the rules of prettiness, she just did not seem aware of them. She took prizes at the end of every school year and gave Philip, with his carefully wet-combed hair and tucked-in shirt, a run for his money every time. After Mr. Auger handed her her test with a flourish, she finished scratching her ear, sat down with her 96 and shot Philip a grin. A pretty grin, if a grin can be pretty.

Celeste was friendly competition. She shared her tests with Philip and showed him where she picked up points. Sometimes they studied together at lunch time. Celeste's ink-stained hands and wholesome smell of bread (she worked at her family's bakery after school) did not distract Philip the way a pretty girl might.

Though Philip had only come in second place on the algebra test, it was him that Mr. Auger pulled aside after class, not Celeste, and said, "You have a good mind for math, have you thought about going to engineering school?"

Philip had a flash of the engineer on the 3:20 train, waving from high up in his seat. That kind of an engineer?

"Civil engineering, or mechanical? Do you like machinery?"

"I've been thinking about learning to be a machinist at the mill."

"Well, you think about engineering. There's a program at the state college. A smart fellow like you should be able to win a scholarship. It would be a shame to see you end up in the mill." Mr. Auger rested his hand on Philip's shoulder and Philip squirmed under its weight.

"Reach for the stars," Mr. Auger said. Then, to peg down the poetry of that, he boxed Philip's shoulder lightly and said, "Go get that sheepskin, okay, son?" To Philip's wondering look, he added, "That's a nickname for a college diploma. A sheepskin."

Reach for the stars. What good was all his studying if he was only aiming for the mill? Philip's short daydream of a machinist's paychecks flew down the hall and out the front doors of the school, leaving him with a new dream. College. He had never felt this way before, this sense that he could rise up out of the valley through his own effort. A scholarship. Why hadn't he ever thought of that?

He stood in the hallway staring down at the worn wooden floorboards and tried to see himself as a college man. A new blue suit, starched white shirt, books under his arm, walking across an endless green lawn. And someone beside him. This person was shadowy, just a presence, but made him feel less alone in the endless green of college.

Philip found Celeste in the lunch room. They compared their algebra tests. He claimed that he'd been careless (better to be careless than stupid) and she brushed his excuses away like dusting flour from her hands. They drilled each other in Latin. He was good at Latin. It was easy to relax into it, knowing that, with the exception of the Latin teacher, Mr. Greeley, no one would ever ask him about it again in his entire life. Celeste had a way of puffing out one cheek when she concentrated, the way a hunting dog lifts a jowl when he's eager to get at a scent. Soft swirls of fine brown hair, too short to be caught up in her ponytail, curled around her ears. Philip took note of these things the way he noticed that her Latin book still had uncut pages in the back. She gave him a molasses cookie, a day-old from the bakery. He remembered Chet saying once, "She's sweet on you."

But she didn't act like girls do when they're sweet on a boy. She made fun of his tiny handwriting and gloated in a friendly way when she beat him on tests. Celeste was sweet on algebra, Latin, biology – not on him. Still, as he sat and watched her lick the nub of her pen and wrap her foot around a chair leg, he kept returning to the daydream that Mr. Auger had started in his head. The endless lawn of the college. The presence that walked beside him became clearer – books under her arm, a ragged ponytail. Who else but Celeste Lavoie would be beside him on that long walk? He tried to picture a pretty girl strolling along – Marie Tate or even a movie star – but it was too much of an effort. When the endless lawn of college rose up behind his eyelids, it was Celeste, with her big French nose, walking along beside him.

"Say, Celeste – are you thinking you'll go to college?"

She looked at him, startled, and forced a laugh.

"Of course not."

"You should. You're smart."

She shrugged and sang Woody Guthrie's song, badly off-key, "If you haven't got the dough-re-me, boys . . ."

"What about a scholarship?"

She shook her head firmly. "That just pays tuition. You have to live someplace, buy meals, books."

And clothes, Philip added silently.

"Besides, I need to help out at the bakery. Et tu, amici?"

"Me? Heck, no. It's like Woody says – you gotta have the dough-re-me." He shrugged to say he didn't care, caught himself hitching up one shoulder, holding it there just like Pa. He was glad he hadn't told his dream to this practical baker's daughter, who sat across from him scrunching up her mouth and working at an equation, as though any of it mattered.

The bell rang. Celeste grabbed her books and ran to her next class. Philip stood up slowly. Two dreams gone in one day. The other students streamed out the door to their afternoon classes. Philip trudged after them. The boy ahead of him, a short, stocky freshman, dropped a piece of paper and Philip bent to pick it up. It was just a chewing gum card with a picture of a ship on the front. He flipped it over. *British Warship At Sea F-L-A-S-H WAR NEWS No. 121 Save to Complete an Entire Collection!* Across the bottom of the card, in red letters: *Can America Maintain Peace with THE WORLD IN ARMS?*

Philip looked at the picture again. A tiny British sailor stood on deck, looking through a pair of binoculars. Two other sailors stood nearby.

"Excuse me." It was the stubby freshman, looking scared but determined. "That's mine."

Philip tossed him the card. The boy snatched it in mid-air and broke out in a big smile, glad Philip wasn't going to make him fight for it. "Gee, thanks!" He started to unbuckle his book bag. "I've got some doubles. I'll give you one."

But Philip had already turned away. The boy watched, puzzled, as Philip marched down the hall past all the class-rooms, and walked right out the front door.

PHILIP RAN ALL THE WAY down Main Street, his breath frosting in the cold. He turned the corner, ran along the high board fence behind his house, then flung open the gate, the iron latch so cold it burned his fingers. He walked quickly across the yard leaving a straight line of brown footprints in the white frost. The hens pecked and scratched at the frozen ground in front of the shed where he had once spent a bitter day of Thanksgiving.

Their clothes hung on the line, scrubbed clean and frozen stiff, waiting for the sun to work its way over the roof peak. Then the door, his hand on the tongue of the latch now, that click that said another one home.

His mother was standing at the sink, bent-over, tired – was everyone always tired here? – she turned and nodded at his shoes –

"Take them off, I just washed the floor."

He bent to unlace his shoes and the moment to announce his decision was gone. Instead, he stood in his stocking feet on the cold, damp floor and faced her as she peeled potatoes.

As he told her, she rinsed the potatoes one by one and dropped them in the pot so he had to keep raising his voice above the sound of running water and potatoes thunking against tin.

"You're too young," she said when he finished.

"They'll take me. We need the money. Look at this place, Ma."

She stared him in the face. "We've been poor a long time. It's never bothered you before."

"I just need Pa to sign for me. I'm underage."

She shook her head. "You go right ahead and ask him."

She turned back to the sink, poured more water over the potatoes, left him standing in his damp socks. He walked past the little sitting room. May was there holding a red ribbon up to the gray light from the window.

"Guess what, May? I'm joining the Navy."

She looked at him and smiled. She laid the ribbon on the arm of the chair and ran her fingertips back and forth on the shiny fabric. He walked upstairs, lay across his bed and opened his history book. It had no meaning anymore, all those old, long-ago wars. There was only the future, bright and clean. He thought of the recruiter, Jimmy Capwell, a valley boy just like himself. He closed his eyes and remembered Jimmy's white uniform, the shiny buttons and gold threads in the stripes and anchors, the rich heft of the starched cloth. He woke to the back door banging and feet on the stairs. The square of gray sky outside his window had gone black.

This was his moment. Groggy, chilly, his socks still damp. He licked his sticky tongue across his teeth and rolled off the bed.

When he was a kid and thought about his future, he imagined it would be revealed to him all at once, like opening a package in the mail. He hoped he would be a lucky fellow and find a good future in that package, that he'd be admired by girls and men and make his mother proud. Now he knew that the future would not come to him. If he waited, all he would get was the mill and a bar on payday. If that. Men were laid off every week lately.

Now he knew that he had to make his future. He had had no idea how, knew no one who had done it. Look at Ruby, with all her dreams come down to lazy Emil Fortin. Then he'd looked at that chewing gum card and remembered the sign Jimmy Capwell had posted in the window of what used to be the shoe store. The US Navy. All he had to do was give them his body. He felt a rush of gratitude for his sturdy arches and sharp eyes, no hernia, no clubfoot, no fainting spells. He tightened the muscles in his stomach and whumped himself right above the belt. He would join the Navy and they'd give him a clean, white uniform and a steady job. All he had to do was get Pa to sign.

"You're a fool!" Pa banged his fist on the piece of paper as though he would drive it through the table. He had been drinking. Philip knew he should have waited until he was sober. When he was like this, Pa would go from weeping to rage, spinning like a weathercock.

"You're not joining any Navy. You're just a kid."

Pa just wanted him stuck at home, under his thumb, Philip thought. But it was useless to argue. He quietly took the recruiter's piece of paper and tucked it into his pocket. A coward, that's what he was. How could he think about joining the Navy when he was such a coward?

Only later, lying on his bed, trying to ignore his hunger – he would not go back down to the kitchen for supper – did he think of ways it might have gone differently. A straight-arm blow to the whiskery chin, standing over him, his foot on his chest. Sign it. Sign it, you son-of-a-bitch. If he was not such a coward. Or he should have waited until morning when Pa was sober. He should have mentioned the money first, the monthly paycheck. Told him what the recruiter said, standing in the old empty shoe store. "The Navy's not going out of business." He should have begged. He should have grabbed him in an arm lock like a champion wrestler, bent him over the table and made him sign. Those and a hundred other ways to remake the past because he could not face the fact that his bright white future was gone.

There was a knock on his door. Ruby.

"What do you want?" He hated her, hated everything in the valley.

She ignored his look. "Did you go to that recruiter in town?"

"Where else would I go?"

"To the base in South County."

"What good will that do?"

"They won't know you from Adam. Jimmy Capwell knows everybody's business here."

"I still have to be seventeen. Or get Pa to sign."

"Lie to them."

"Who told you this?"

"Emil's pal Frenchie. They took him down in South County. After he was turned down here. You know how he gets those little spells sometimes? From a fever when he was a kid?"

"Does Frenchie think we're going to join the war?" *Can America Maintain Peace with THE WORLD IN ARMS?*

"Nobody does. We don't need to go all the way to Europe to find problems, we've got plenty of problems right here. Everyone knows that."

"That's what Jimmy Capwell said, too."

The next morning Philip bounded out of bed, then paced the floor – eight steps across, back and forth – until he heard the door slam and saw Pa walking across the yard in the rain. Then he heard his mother climbing the stairs, her heavy body, heard her standing outside his door catching her breath.

"You in there?"

Where else would I be? he felt himself sneer, and wondered if he would ever forgive her for taking Pa's side against him in this.

"You going to school today?"

"No." He heard her huff, then her slow, heavy steps down to the kitchen. She knew not to try to make him go. She knew he had started to slip away from her already. He was a regular Harry Houdini, working his way out of everything that tied him down to this dreary old place. He dressed and went downstairs.

"Where's Pa's old boots?"

"What do you want them for?"

"My shoes are wet." It is so easy to lie. How old are you? Seventeen, sir.

He put on the thick-soled boots. They were worn, but still had a good inch of heel. Unless the recruiter was very tall, he'd have to look up at him in these boots. They were too loose, so he shoved some pages from his school notes into the toes. He wouldn't need them again. He swallowed a big lump of sadness when he thought about that, but there was nothing to be done about it.

He slicked his hair straight back, then put a little hair oil on it because it was fighting to lie back into his schoolboy side-part. He stood in the big boots, taller than he'd ever been – glad now for his long legs. He squared his shoulders, watched his lips in the mirror. Seventeen, sir. Dropped his voice. Seventeen sir.

Emil took him as far as he could on the back of his Indian, but had to turn around to get to work on time. Then a farmer took him the rest of the way. He sat in the farmer's truck, bursting with lies to tell him, wanting to practice before he got to the recruiter. But the farmer was not a talkative man, just grunted to Philip's comments about the rain.

It went the way Ruby said it would go.

"Seventeen, sir."

A half-an-hour later he stood in the rain on the side of the road just beyond the guard shack outside the base. Grinning like a fool, he knew it. The first car that came by pulled over for him, a big Packard sedan with dark-red velvet seats. Life was already getting better. The driver was comfortably fat and wore a suit and tie.

"I just joined the Navy!" He sounded like a kid to his own ears but it didn't matter anymore. He had enlisted. He was getting a white uniform.

"You don't say! You're smart to enlist, before they draft you."

"Draft me?"

"Soon as we get into the war, there'll be a big draft just like the Great War."

"You think we're going to join the war?"

"You can bet your bottom dollar on it, sonny. I'm thinking that Roosevelt, Churchill, all them big shots, are talking it over right now. Yes, indeed." He nodded, his soft chin rolling over his stiff white collar. It seemed like a damp wind had blown into the car, but Philip was not going to let it snuff out his joy. The fat man smiled.

"Hey, sailor! That calls for a celebration. Open that glove compartment."

Philip found a silver flask and small cups. The car rode so smoothly, he could pour without spilling.

"Whoa there, boy! That's expensive stuff you're pouring."

Philip sniffed. The whiskey had a nice smoky smell. He took a sip and almost spit it out, it was so nasty. It scalded all the way down. He took another sip, expecting the burn this time, and managed to hold it in his mouth for a minute before swallowing slowly. He did not like the taste, but liked the warm feeling that rose up in his chest. The man reached over and slapped his shoulder.

"Kentucky bourbon. The best there is."

Philip sank back into the soft seat, sipping the good bourbon out of a little silver cup. It took the edge off the doubt that started to whittle at his happiness when the man talked about the war. Everything was shining now, including him. This was his new life. It was going to be swell. The rain stopped just before the man dropped him off outside of town. He said he was driving all the way to Hartford, Connecticut. "Good luck, sailor!"

He had pictured showing up at the bakery in his new uniform, but as he walked by he saw it was open and decided to go in and tell Celeste. A little bell above the door jingled when he stepped inside, and it made him jump. The glow of the bourbon had worn off during the long walk into town. A woman came out of the back room, wiping her hands on a big white apron. She had gray eyes like Celeste, but hers were hard and shrewd.

"Is Celeste here?"

She looked him up and down, deciding, then called "Celeste!" She didn't take her small eyes off him until Celeste came out, as though he might break the glass case and reach in to steal a cream horn or an éclair. He was relieved when she went into the back room, leaving Celeste to guard the pastries. She was surprised to see him.

"I came by because I've enlisted. In the Navy. I wanted to tell you."

"Gee. That's swell. I guess that's real swell."

She looked like she wanted to say more, raised her hand as though she wanted to shake hands with him or maybe just touch him. But the counter was between them like a big white iceberg.

"I'll be leaving in a couple of weeks."

"You won't graduate!"

"Guess not." He shrugged, one shoulder hitching up and hanging there. "You'll win all the prizes now."

She stared at him, with a bit of her mother's hardness coming into her eyes, like he'd broken a promise. She opened her mouth to say something, but the door banged wide and the tiny bell clanged. A woman came in carrying a crying toddler.

"Stop it now, and Momma will buy you a sweet!"

Celeste shifted her eyes to the back room, to the woman with the squalling child, then back to Philip.

"Looks like you've got paying customers," he said. "So long." He backed out the door, watching Celeste duck down behind the counter to bag up sweets for the crying child.

MABEL FELT HIM AWAKE beside her, his legs moving and twitching as though they were something apart from him, raring to get up and walk for miles. The rest of him had to be tired, all those long hours in the mill, standing there day after day. He was a steady worker, thank God for that.

He was worrying, she knew, about Philip. Wondering if he'd done right by not signing the recruiter's paper. She lay still, her body tense, not sure if she should touch him, say something, or leave him to thrash it out on his own. He was a hard man to read.

He stirred and she turned, her hand ready to reach for him. But he quietly slipped out of bed and her empty hand fell back to the bed sheet. She heard his feet, soft on the stairs. She drifted off for a moment, then woke to music. He was playing his fiddle, a slow, gentle tune in the night. He had not played the fiddle in a long time. He didn't take it with him anymore when he went out in the evenings, said no one wanted those old-fashioned songs anymore. It stayed locked in its old, black case, the leather worn rough at the edges, red as clay. He was probably right. The old songs were sweet music for a sweeter time.

She listened as he played, the tune going quietly round and round, the high notes faltering. The old fiddle must be out of tune, she thought, shut up in its case for so long. He had been right not to sign their son away to the Navy. Not with Hitler on the loose over in Europe, no matter what everyone said. She thought of her brother Omer, everyone's happy-go-lucky favorite, when he returned home from the Great War. Never the same, her mother always said. At least his body was whole, not like some of the other boys. The part of him that was broken was inside and could not be seen. But she remembered other boys and the brief hush that came over the crowd when they came off the train. Boys without legs, without faces. That hush – one breath – then someone would start them all cheering again, louder, to make up for that one bit of silence.

She shook her head in the dark. Philip was angry at them now, but someday he would understand.

Come back to bed and sleep now, she thought, for you've done right. Money was dear, but he had refused to sell their son. She felt a flash of pride. Yes, this time, he'd done right. The music downstairs ended on one long, soft note, like a sigh. Again, she heard his steps on the stairs, lighter now. She closed her eyes and waited for sleep. Maybe as soon as tomorrow, Philip would begin to understand.

EARLY SPRING, 1940. Once again, the lights are going out all over world. In France and Belgium, in the Orient, in the deserts of North Africa.

Philip is taking a walk along the dirt road that cuts across the face of the hills above the valley. He's not one to go for a walk usually, and never by himself. Why go alone when you can be with a pal? But all day the valley has been too narrow, and this walk feels like coming up for air. Monday he'll take the train to Boston and report for duty. He likes the sound of that, of his life moving, sixteen years – a long time, he thinks – stalled in this stalled town and now, to report for duty.

The dirt road winds ahead of him, even and smooth as a velvet ribbon. The woods on either side are open, last year's leaves dark on the ground. Tree trunks on the hillside above him stand thin and black, like ink marks on paper. Stubborn oak leaves still cling to the higher branches. On the other side of the road, the land falls away into the valley. He hears only his breath, his shoes hitting the ground, the call of a crow winging over the hillside. He is leaving it all. Leaving, leaving his heels say as they hit the hard-packed dirt. All the trees on this side of the valley are thin young saplings. Woodcutters have hauled out the old trees felled by the terrible hurricane of 1938, leaving a forest of young trees bent by the weight of last winter's ice. The stumps of the old trees are thick and black with rain.

Philip walks with his head down, hands jammed into the pockets of his jacket, his shoes hitting the ground in a marching rhythm. Soon it will be chin up, eyes straight ahead. He smiles. Things are suddenly moving so fast. Already, all that he knows – the streets of the town, the sound of the mill and the river in spring flood, the book knowledge so carefully learned, all those Latin verbs and algebra equations. None of it matters. The thinness of the soles of his shoes, his wrists sticking out of the cuffs of his jacket. None of it. He is free of it all. There is a new self waiting for him in Boston. A man strong and confident, never afraid. He sees this self, like an older brother, beckoning.

But now his mother's face rises up, her broad face with the three deep lines between her brows. She keeps giving him things. A black comb, a white handkerchief, a pair of woolen socks. "You might need this." They weigh him down, her small gifts, they tether him to this place. He needs nothing now, the time for that has gone. Let them shear off his hair, take his shabby clothes, forge him in the fire like new metal.

Her broad worried face, her eyes that ask: What have you done? She remembers the Great War, but these are different times. He shrugs, though there is no one to see him flick war off his shoulder and into the weed-choked ditch. He knows what everyone knows. America helped them before and now they're at it again. Like a fight between school yard bullies. You don't get mixed up in it, you walk away. But even as he whispered this – just walk away – he felt it – War – the way the hurricane had brought the salt smell of the sea miles overland to the valley.

He reached the place in the road where it turned sharply and climbed. He stopped and stood there for a while, feeling his sweat dry, cooling his back and chest. The sun was setting. Three crows rose from a huge elm and moved across the hillside, dark and quiet as cloud shadows. He looked down into the town. The mill standing like a black fortress, the white steeple of St. John the Baptist, and the river through it all like a twisted band of steel. Down there, his pals were running in from the outfield in time for supper. Celeste was locking the door of the bakery. Everyone was hurrying home, those awaited and those going home alone to empty houses.

Goodbye. An exultant goodbye, his life flying up in a widening circle over the valley. Leaving so that he could return. Return changed, return new. The sun set, leaving a narrow band of pale yellow under a dark bank of clouds. Lights were going on all over the valley. Warm golden squares of light and for the first time he felt a rush of love for it all, tears cool and wet on his lashes. He gave a cheer, a half-choked cry. Early spring, 1940 – the lights going on, all over the valley – and Philip is leaving his father's house.

MY FATHER WENT TO SEA and lived through two wars, World War II and the Korean Conflict. But he never told war stories. It is hard for me to think of him fighting in a war. For all his fury at home, out in the world he was not a fighting man. He was a happy-go-lucky man who enjoyed his comforts, sitting in the cool dimness of a bar on a hot summer afternoon watching a ball game on TV. He mentioned once that on shipboard they had to wash their clothes with salt water and how he hated that, how it made him feel dirty and itchy. He had a redhead's skin, sensitive and easily irritated.

One summer, my brothers spent every day playing War in the woods behind our house. They raced up and down the paths, hid behind rocks and oak trees and tossed pine cone grenades. The man next door, Mr. Fallon, father of daughters but no sons, called them into his garage one day and showed them his old Army gear. Genuine military stuff. An ammo box, a metal helmet, a stinking canvas pup tent. He gave them all of it. Until then, War had been just a game, played with stick rifles and cap pistols, like Cowboys and Indians. Mr. Fallon's heavy green gear made them feel the realness of war, made them understand it was a game they might play themselves someday.

But Mr. Fallon had been in the Army for only two years, stationed in Alabama, where it was hot but not dangerous. He had never been in a war. Maybe he told them to ask their dad. Maybe it just occurred to them that they had a real player sitting right in the living room watching the Red Sox on TV.

One night, they asked him, squirming like puppies, "What was the war like, Dad?"

I stopped reading my book and listened for his answer. I waited for some brave story about how he saved a ship. He never seemed to know that kids can sense a lie even when they can't imagine the truth.

His answer: "War is being on a boat watching ships get blown out of the water and knowing your buddies are on them." It was clear there were to be no more questions. My brothers shuffled down the hall to their room, where I heard them talking quietly about baseball. They took down Mr. Fallon's pup tent the next day.

I have told that story again and again. One of my father's finest moments. A time when he told the truth, a time he had something to teach and did it well. That night, I remember sitting in the living room, the crickets and katydids singing in the bushes outside, trying to picture what my father said.

I imagined blackness, the open sea at night, the orange glare of a fireball. But I could not imagine how it would feel to know that people I knew and liked, my best friend or my science teacher, were in the midst of that fireball. Unthinkable. I was a lucky kid who did not know death very well. Animals hit by cars, old relatives I'd never met, strangers on the TV news. I pictured my father across time, a young sailor on a big battleship in a warm Pacific night, on the winning side of the Good War. He had joined the Navy to defend America, was glad to do his duty. I saw him watching death from a long distance across the water, safe aboard a ship that made it home. I saw him as a lucky one, a watcher, alone but unhurt. It was hard to imagine the buddies he had talked about. He didn't have any friends that I knew of, and I wondered if those Navy buddies were the last friends he had.

I was wrong about all of it, except his aloneness. One of his cousins knew the name of the ship he served on in World War II. During the war years, that cousin was about the same age as my brothers were when they were so eager for my father's war stories. More than fifty years later, at my mother's funeral, I could see the hero worship in his old eyes as he told us the story my father would not tell.

My father served in the cold North Atlantic, not the Pacific, as I had always assumed. He was not on a battleship. He was a sailor on the Sapelo, an oiler, a small ship that carried flammable fuel. Sapelo AO-11, known as Lucky 'Leven.

AO-11 was part of Convoy ONS-5, Iceland to New York Harbor, mainly supply ships that carried fuel and ammunition. The convoy was discovered by a German submarine group midway through its journey. The weather was clear, with good visibility. Nazi U-boats were able to pick off one ship after another, like players at some grisly carnival game. Day after day, the convoy limped toward New York, harried by the Nazis. One, two, three ships less each day. "War is being on a boat watching ships get blown out of the water and knowing your buddies are on them." Men – boys – overboard, flailing in the icy water, burning in flaming oil slicks. Thirteen of the original forty-three ships in the convoy went down. After six days, fog rolled in and the convoy no longer provided easy targets for the U-boats. Sapelo AO-11 got its nickname, Lucky 'Leven, and young Seaman Philip Paul made it home.

Years later, I find a photo of ol' Lucky 'Leven in a Navy archive. A graceless, gray metal ship. AO-11 Sapelo. 447 feet long, 60-foot beam. AO-11 is one ship of many in this archive. There is nothing outstanding about it. A note below the photo – a short write-up about Convoy ONS-5 – gives a date and place to the only words I ever heard my father say about any of his war experiences.

I look at the date and put it together with the year of my father's underage enlistment. For the first time, I realize that he joined the Navy before the United States entered the war. I had always assumed that my father, caught up in the patriotic fervor of the times, enlisted to join the war effort. But Americans rallied to the war effort after the attack on Pearl Harbor. When my father joined the Navy at the age of sixteen, the average person on the street did not believe America should ever again cross the Atlantic to go to war.

I imagine blackness, the open sea at night. He is standing at the metal rail of the Sapelo, before it became the Lucky 'Leven. His hands are cracked and bleeding in the bitter cold, his wrists skinny and bare below the filthy cuffs of his seaman's jacket. Even on deck, he cannot get away from the stench of oil. He is eighteen. He still has freckles across the bridge of his nose. I see him alone, watching. There is another ship out there, a dark shape keeping pace with his.

I QUIT COLLEGE IN my junior year. The whole country was in the middle of a recession, and a college diploma was a worthless piece of paper. The newspapers were full of interviews with cabdrivers and waitresses who had English and engineering degrees. College had served its purpose, gotten me away from my father's house. Getting there had been an end in itself, and after a few aimless semesters of late-night parties, I was restless and adrift.

I took the money I had saved for tuition, bought a twelve-year-old Pontiac station wagon and took a job in one of the few working ports left in New England, cutting flounder and shucking clams. My plan was to save enough money to travel around the country for a year. I wanted to get out of New England.

Once my plans were set, I drove to my parents' house to show them the old car and give them my news. Though it was cold and drizzling, I drove with the windows down so I could listen to the car's engine, hoping all that noise meant it was ready for a continent's worth of miles.

My father was home, showered and spruce, ready to leave for work at three, the evening shift at the factory. He had been promoted to shift supervisor and liked to get in early to set a good example for his workers. So I told him quickly and as casually as I could about college and my new plans. I was twenty-one, an adult. I was not asking for permission, I was telling him my intentions.

"You're wasting your life," he said quietly. I shrugged. I had paid for my broken-off education. My life was mine to waste. He didn't yell or rage, just turned his head and stared out the window, like he was watching something fall out of the sky.

The next time I stopped by, he had his own news. He had bought a new house near Narragansett Bay. "My retirement house," he said. "We might even get a boat." I was surprised. He had never shown any liking for the ocean, despite his years in the Navy, and had always joked that he would never set foot on a boat smaller than a battleship. Now he was buying a house on an island and thinking of owning a little runabout.

My mother was excited and showed me snapshots of the house, which was still being built. It was a graceful, cedar-shingled house with white shutters. The roof sloped down in back from the second floor. "A traditional Colonial saltbox house," my father said proudly. He told me he had stopped by the day before and found the builder hand-sanding the hardwood floors. My father mentioned wall-to-wall carpeting to him, his idea of luxury.

"The guy stands up, throws down his tools, and says he's not going to finish the job if I'm just going to cover it up with cheap rugs. He's a real craftsman type." My father held up his hands. "Okay, okay, I says to him – forget the rugs!" It was the first time I had known him to admit that someone else might be right. My father laughed, embarrassed at his lack of taste and proud of his hardwood floors. But I just smiled. Who could laugh at him, this poor-boy with his new hand-crafted house?

They moved to the new house in spring. It had a stone fireplace with a wooden mantle, two bathrooms, a sunny deck out back. I walked through the clean, airy rooms and marveled that my parents lived in them. They stood together in the empty dining room and discussed how big a table they would need, then measured the floor space. It was the first time I had ever heard them have a discussion that did not end in shouts and tears. It was as though the salt air had cleansed something between them.

"Come by on weekends," my father said. "Bring your friends. We can have cook-outs on the deck. Maybe your brothers will come now, too." He had bought a set of lawn darts. It was set up in the back yard and he wanted to show me how to play. I felt like I was living some other girl's life. It looked like a good life, but I already had my own. I did not want to spend all afternoon playing lawn darts with him and said I had plans. He walked me out to my station wagon.

"If you decide to go back to college in the fall, you can come live here. It's not that far, and we've got plenty of room." He stood there, happy and expectant. I told him thanks, but I'd be traveling in the fall. I did not say that even this beautiful, airy, new house could never bring me home again.

Later that spring, my father was laid off by the factory, or maybe fired. He never said which. He was one year short of retirement. When he applied for insurance on the mortgage for the new house, he was refused after the medical examination. He never said why. He stopped wearing his watch, that long-ago gift from my brothers, and shook and flicked his hands as though they were numb. My mother told me all this when I stopped by after work or on weekends, in quick, whispered statements as I was walking out the door. What she did not mention was his drinking.

Drink had always seemed to fuel my father. It made him even bigger, redder, and more unpredictable, like a volcano. But now the drink consumed him. He spent all his time in the tiny den of their new house, sitting on the couch in a gray fog of cigarette smoke, the TV buzzing. He was usually shirtless and his skin was gray as though drained of blood. He seemed to shrink from the inside. The skin under his chin hung empty, his swollen belly looked hollow. His big arms were like sticks, the skin hanging slack above his elbows. His thick gleaming hair went dry, brittle and totally gray.

All his life, he had been a beer drinker. Beer seemed like a friendly drink, part of picnics and ball games. Though the truth was, after he stopped going out to bars, my father drank alone. The brown bottles that gathered on the kitchen counter were at least familiar, with their bright red and blue labels. Now I watched him sit with a glass filled with a colorless liquid – cheap vodka – that he gulped as though it was a job. If there had ever been joy in his drinking, it was gone now. This drinking left him stranded on the couch, sleeping and waking, drifting off again.

Before the colorless liquid, he had always kept the polished appearance of a Navy man. No matter what shape he was in at night – if he had burned dollar bills in an ashtray at midnight or splattered soup on the kitchen walls – the next morning he'd be sitting with the newspaper, his ruddy face close-shaven and shining. Now, in the blur between his nights and his days, he did not bother to shave. The stubble on his face and neck was white.

He had always been quick and light on his feet, surprising for a man of his size. He loved to dance, once mentioned how he and his sister used to practice the foxtrot in the kitchen, humming the tunes because they could not afford a radio. Even in middle age, with his body swollen by years of drinking, he had carried himself with a dancer's grace. Now he was a lurching gray wreck. He would stand, steadying himself with one hand on the TV, when I walked into the den to say goodbye.

"Can you loan me a ten, just 'til the check comes in?" he'd ask softly, looking out toward the kitchen, where my mother sat at the table staring at the back yard. The first time, I made him promise that he would not spend it on drink. It gave me a strange sense of power. But it was an ugly kind of power, to know I was but one of his masters.

The vodka owned him now, as though it had finally caught him hopeless and adrift, and placed a cold hand on his shoulder to steer him. The next time I just handed him the money. I never expected to see it again.

But at some point, the check did come in and he paid me back. "Buy yourself something nice," he said. I bought two retread tires for my car.

Though he was so changed, I did not worry about him. He was not like other men. My father was indestructible. He was never sick, never wore a hat or gloves no matter the weather. Nothing hurt him. He smoldered, he blew up, he did the damage then walked out the door.

I knew that one day he would get off the couch and find a job, and this summer of gray idleness would never be mentioned again. I did worry about my mother, about her life with this man. This ghost-father, living off unemployment checks for the first time in his life. But I had always worried about her.

"I don't know how much longer this can go on," was all she would say. She seemed restless in the new house and found fault with it. She showed me a crack that had appeared at the foot of the driveway. She said the soil in the back yard was dry and the grass kept dying. I pulled up my father's lawn darts and set up a sprinkler.

One afternoon when I stopped by after work, my father was not in the den. For a moment my heart soared, then my mother told me he had been admitted to Newport Naval Hospital. He had fallen in the front yard that morning and was taken away by ambulance. She said she didn't know what was wrong with him and would not talk about what led up to the call for the ambulance.

"They came and took him away," was all she said. She spoke as though he had been abducted. I phoned her the next day and he was still in the hospital. She did not seem concerned, said he would probably be home soon. The next day I worked a double shift and my car ran out of gas on the way home. It turned out that the car had a leaky gas pump and I was busy dealing with that, worried it might postpone my trip. My mother called to say my father was still in the hospital. She said she did not know why they would not send him home. She said their next door neighbors wanted to visit him, but she did not want them there. I asked if he was allowed visitors. "Only family," she said. "I just want family."

My brother had been to see him and had brought him a plant, she told me. "But I don't think the hospital allows plants," she said. "They're not like civilian hospitals," she explained with a note of pride. I was surprised that my brother had visited and realized I should probably visit him, too. Despite the distance between us, he was my father and he was in the hospital. But my car was in the shop. Another day slid by before I went to see him.

It was July 17, 1976. Newport was celebrating America's Bicentennial Year and there was a long line at the toll booth for the Newport Bridge. The Tall Ships were anchored in Newport Harbor and their sailors, young men from all over the world, filled the streets in their dress whites and caps. I drove through crowds of revelers to the security gate at the Navy base. The guard saluted and waved me through, and I drove past trim green lawns to the hospital.

After the glare of the July sun, the dim, cool hospital corridors felt like being underwater. The hospital's military austerity was familiar and comforting. We were a Navy family. My father had been in the Navy for twenty years and plain white buildings like this one had always served us well.

He was in a room by himself. Even then, so diminished, he looked too big for the narrow bed and was straining against the tight, starched sheets. He twitched and threw his limbs around. I stood at the foot of the bed and waited for him to wake and recognize me. A clean-cut orderly, who did not look much older than me, came in and tried to give my father his medication. My father had been retired from the Navy for fifteen years, so it was odd to hear him addressed by rank and surname.

"C'mon, Paul. Take it easy now, Chief."

My father refused the medication. Without opening his eyes, he tightened his lips and tossed his head like a nervous horse. The young orderly was vexed but deferential to my father, who, though semi-conscious and in a hospital gown, out-ranked him. Finally, he handed me the cup and said, "Maybe he'll take it for you."

I was surprised that he assumed I had any influence over my father. But I offered to try, and he left the room. The cup contained a grainy white liquid, like aspirins crushed in milk. I put the tiny paper cup to my father's lips and he took a sip. I encouraged him and he swallowed the rest. The orderly had been right, after all.

The medicine seemed to quiet him, and he slept. His breathing filled the room as it had filled our house through the nights of my childhood. I remembered how he had always been a loud and restless sleeper, given to sudden shouts and teeth-grinding. Now he seemed almost docile in the starched white sheets, his mouth slightly open, each breath slow and deep.

I sat in a plastic visitor's chair with my legs drawn up onto the seat. I was wearing cut-off jeans and my sunburned legs were sticky against the plastic. He seemed deeply asleep. I leafed through an old news magazine and wondered how long I needed to stay, how soon I could decently leave. Outside the window, the hard summer sky softened into late afternoon. A robin ruffled its feathers in the spray of a lawn sprinkler. My father's hair against the pillow was longish and tousled, like a boy's.

Out in the hallway, dinner carts rattled and cushioned soles squeaked on the polished floors. In my father's room, an empty space between breaths grew longer.

There is a breath that is the last, audible and nourishing like all the others before it. Finally, I understood there would not be another.

I ran into the hallway and called for help, part of me not believing it was a real emergency. I was surprised at how swiftly a doctor and his orderlies appeared. They ordered me out of the room and, with practiced efficiency, wheeled in big shiny machines as though it was indeed an emergency.

I stood outside the door and listened. The doctor gave orders in stern, clipped phrases with the double authority of medicine and the military. There were mechanical whirrings, an electronic hum, then a loud crackling explosion.

"Wake up, Paul. Come around, Chief!"

The doctor sounded as though he would order my father back to consciousness. There was another explosion. More commands to the orderlies, louder and more frantic. Then, with his machines failing, his expertise failing, the doctor fell back on an old method of waking sleepers who are slipping away. He called to my father.

"Chief? Paul?" He was crying, this doctor was crying. "PAUL!"

It did not occur to me to call him, that my voice – Dad! – might have brought him back. In any event, I am not sure I could have called to him then with the sincere desperation of that doctor.

The doctor came to the doorway and beckoned me into the room. He shook his head and said something I did not hear. The room, which had been so neat and precise, looked like a battlefield. The machines were askew and unplugged. The bewildered orderlies filed past me in their rumpled white uniforms. The doctor wiped his eyes with his sleeve and followed them.

My father was lying on the bed like he had been thrown from a great height. They had pulled a sheet across him, perhaps tried to arrange his limbs so he would look peaceful to me. His eyes were closed.

I reached out and touched his cheek, something I had not done since I was a small child. It was cold and hard, like a rock. I knew what I was supposed to feel, what a daughter should feel when her father is dead. But I felt only relief. I remembered the times I had woken in the night to him raging through the house and how I had wished him gone. Now he was gone. I whispered goodbye and walked out the door.

The doctor and his disheveled orderlies stood in the hall, scuffing their white shoes on the linoleum. They seemed to be steeling themselves for my reproaches and tears. I walked past them, dry-eyed and calm. They were blameless. How could they have hauled him back when he'd been drifting away for years?

THAT DAY HIS FACE was pressed against the grass but he could not smell it. Only feel that it was cool against his skin. He was going out to the car. He remembered the car keys jingling in his shaking hand. Now his hand was empty. His watch was gone, too, he could feel it missing – hey, my boys gave me that watch! But no, he had stopped wearing the watch, it made his hand numb. Something was wrong with his hands lately. But he could still drive. He was going out to buy beer. No, not beer, that didn't work anymore. Vodka. Vodka still worked, he needed it now, could imagine a long sip sliding down his throat. But he was on the grass.

"Sir? What happened? Are you okay? Are you okay, sir?"

"I'm fine." But he wasn't fine, his face was in the grass and no one heard him say he was fine, and there was a loud noise, a siren? A fire? A lot of people around him, telling him not to move. To just stay there. He wasn't trying to go anywhere, just sit up, find his keys.

"Where are my keys?" They did not understand that he just needed to find his keys. "Turn off that noise!" They did, they did that much. They wanted him to lie down, they rolled him over onto his back and his face was not in the grass anymore, it was in the sky. Someone was taking his shoes.

"Leave my shoes alone!"

They were busy, too busy to hear him. Like he wasn't there. Or maybe they weren't there. He hoped they were still there.

"Hey, buddy. Somebody. Find me my keys, I'll buy you a drink."

Then the siren again. Or a train whistle. Something cold on his face and heavy. He could not open his eyes. He was tired. He had lost his keys. He wished they had let him lie with his face in the grass, just a little while longer. It was dark here. Cold and dark.

He was alone.

He was walking down Main Street. A cloudy day, sky heavy as a frying pan. That's what Ma used to say. She used to talk more, smile more, laugh. Lately she was too tired to talk. When he asked her a question – any more potatoes? – she'd just point with her chin at the stove. Her mouth was a hard line under soft cheeks. Maybe she was sick. The thought made him stop right there on Main Street and catch his breath. No, nothing must happen to Ma. It wouldn't be fair, her dying in the middle of such sadness. Her sadness pulled the curtains closed in the kitchen, and boiled the beans until the soft part fell away from the tough woody string that he could not swallow.

What if Ma died? It would be like Sunday after Mass,

when everyone crowded around Father Michaud to shake his hand, eager to show they'd been to church. Philip looked back through the church doors, down the empty aisle. The altar boy, the cuffs of his pants showing under his white gown, stood alone on the altar holding the long-handled candle snuffer. When he reached up and put out the last candle, the church became a big hollow building with mice running along the ceiling beams. Not holy anymore.

Now it's a cold, cloudy day, and the trees are all bare except the oaks, which still hold their tough, brown leaves. Ma once told him that Pa was hard and stubborn because his father had beat him with a stick made of oak. Philip had never met that man, his grandfather. When he thought of him, he imagined a big oak stubbornly clinging to its dead leaves.

The fire is out again. Philip shivers, the wind is coming through the open window. An east wind. The wind that brings cold rain. That is what Ma says, the east wind coming in off the ocean. He has never seen the ocean. The ocean is miles away from the valley.

The ocean is a heaving gray thing that will swallow them all if this ship goes down. For a suit of clothes he has joined the Navy and now there is nowhere to run. Only watch the other ships on the long gray horizon.

The fire is out again, Philip. Go down the dark stairs to the cellar and hope there's still some coal in the scuttle.

He is so cold. The east wind is blowing over him and Ma is calling. "Philip, come on now, it's time to go."

Then he is warm. His eyes are closed and it's quiet, but he knows he is home. At last. He wonders, in that brief moment before opening his eyes, what it will be like, finally, to be home.

SEVERAL WEEKS AFTER my father died, my mother told me about a dream. In her dream, my father was in the hospital and she was afraid he was dying. A doctor walked up to her and told her that he would never die. "Your husband is like the Rock of Gibraltar," the doctor said.

"That's how I always thought of him. Faithful as the Rock of Gibraltar. I can't believe he's gone." We were sitting at the kitchen table, and she held the hem of the tablecloth, smoothing it tenderly, in a way I had never seen her touch my father. I was surprised by her sudden tenderness toward him, my volatile, raging father. I felt a surge of anger and betrayal that she would show love for him now, after all those years of bitterness and complaint. I wondered if there might have been a man I had not known, a father I had missed. But that wondering flashed and died. At twenty-one, it was easier for me to hold onto my familiar anger than question such a complicated loss.

Many years later, my partner and I were helping my mother pack her house to move to an apartment. I found a scarf in the back of a drawer. It was mine, but I had not seen it in since I was a child. It was big and silky, with a bright red border. Inside the border, there were bullfighters, tango-dancers, a Navy battleship and a monkey labeled "The Gibraltar Ape." These all circled around an island, "Gibraltar – The Rock." My father had brought the scarf back from his last overseas trip, just before he left the Navy. I remembered him standing in the kitchen in his uniform, handing out gifts. I was five years old, and the monkey on the scarf was the only thing of interest to me. It was an impractical gift for a young child, and I never wore it.

I looked at the scarf my father had given me so many years ago and remembered my mother's long-ago dream after he died. Her Rock of Gibraltar. I remembered my anger and that flicker of loss. How little time he and I had had together. Twenty-one years, not even that. Lost, the time he was away at sea. Lost, the times he sat silent. Lost, the times I avoided him.

He was not there when I returned to college and graduated with honors. He never met the dark-haired young woman I met there and fell in love with. Years later, when she said, "I wish I could have known your dad, I think I would have liked him," I wondered why. She said that sometimes – when I was generous with money or made sure no one was left out of a good time – she knew I was acting like him. I told her that he would have liked her, and in saying it, knew it was true. He would have looked past all his prejudices to see the joy in my eyes.

I looked at the scarf in my hands. The Gibraltar in the center of the square of silk was not huge and alone as I remembered him, nor was it my mother's faithful rock. This Gibraltar was a green and gold island in an aquamarine sea, with small, white boats sailing in its harbor. Peaceful and bright.

I counted back the years and realized I was the same age my father was when he bought that scarf for me, his young daughter across the Atlantic. My partner and I had been together for a dozen years and I knew the loneliness of being away from her when I occasionally traveled for my work. What was it like for him to be away from home and family, at sea for months at a time? He had always returned to us. The faithfulness and commitment that blessed my life had, perhaps, begun with him.

That day, with my mother growing old, my own hair silver at the temples, as my father's had once been, I thought of him choosing that bright and shiny scarf. I looked down at him from the height of the soothing years and imagined him in the warm sun at a market stall. It's his last trip overseas. He doesn't try to bargain with the market woman, just hands her a fistful of foreign dollars because she's poor and has kids. He smiles and jokes, and she laughs, though they don't speak the same language. He looks sharp in his bright, white uniform – clean-cut, sunburned and still hopeful. Standing there, with all the time in the world, on that gentle, gold island of Gibraltar. Something flickered in me then, a spark. Something that would someday, I hoped, become love.

LaVergne, TN USA
16 November 2009
164255LV00001B/3/P